About the Author

Tobias Yeats is the author of the novels, *Play*, and *Parliament*. He has lived in many countries both discovering and experiencing all kinds of different cultures. He has studied the great architectural classics, sculpture and paintings. He regularly visits the church. He lives in Oxfordshire.

Play

Tobias Yeats

Play

Olympia Publishers
London

www.olympiapublishers.com
OLYMPIA PAPERBACK EDITION

Copyright © Tobias Yeats 2022

The right of Tobias Yeats to be identified as author of
this work has been asserted in accordance with sections 77 and 78 of
the Copyright, Designs and Patents Act 1988.

All Rights Reserved

No reproduction, copy or transmission of this publication
may be made without written permission.
No paragraph of this publication may be reproduced,
copied or transmitted save with the written permission of the publisher,
or in accordance with the provisions
of the Copyright Act 1956 (as amended).

Any person who commits any unauthorised act in relation to
this publication may be liable to criminal
prosecution and civil claims for damage.

A CIP catalogue record for this title is
available from the British Library.

ISBN: 978-1-80074-596-4

This is a work of fiction.
Names, characters, places and incidents originate from the writer's
imagination. Any resemblance to actual persons, living or dead, is
purely coincidental.

First Published in 2022

**Olympia Publishers
Tallis House
2 Tallis Street
London
EC4Y 0AB**

Printed in Great Britain

Dear friends, let us love one another

Chapter 1
Harvey

The largest planned racing day was to commence upon the course and it would turn the course into a vibrant mix of top hats and pageantry. The calendared event made sure that a selection of interesting people journeyed to the city. The stands had become prepared and men on ladders made final preparations to banners and seating, the release stiles were primed and ready to take the horses for the day's events. In the stables beyond, a young boy stood with a pitchfork dressed in tight jodhpurs tucked to his socks and with a thickly woven jumper over a roll-neck upon his thin scrawny neck. The spikey blond-haired boy made his way towards the stable closely followed by his father, Harvey. Together they began to work the hay to the corner of the stable, bundling it into large canvas sacks for convoy. The young boy struggled with the size of his fork and turned towards Harvey, he approached the boy and standing beside him guided the weight of the hay to the collection bag. A squat man with a rounded head and large fiery rounded eyes, his head was balding with galled tufts to its surround.

'There,' he said. 'All complete.' As they bundled the last of the hay from the stable floor. The boy clapped his hands in celebration at the completed task.

'Are we able to go riding now,' the boy said viewing a large white horse with grey mottling upon the stone forecourt.

'We are now able to find time to take a short ride, I am to be sure that I prepare the remainder of the horses for racing.' He reached out to touch his hand to his son's back. 'The two large studs shall race alongside one another today in the headline race,' he said excitedly. The horses in the large stable held their heads at lumber, visible over the stable doors. The pair paused in the yard before one of the large chestnut horses and patted to the side of the horse's neck proudly. He gently brushed with the flat of his hand a piece of hay free that had become caught in the boy's spikey hair. The boy gazed longingly at Harvey. The man's sleeve of his heavy wax jacket revealed a small pale hand that he reached upwards with to steady his flat cap.

He stood before the horse and cupped his hands together. Crouching, he raised his foot to his hands to lift the boy to the saddle. The boy's small hands clutched the horse.

'Be steady with your foot in my hand.' He lifted the boy up and over the horse. 'Up you go.' The boy grabbed at the firm leather saddle with his hand. The boy had ridden the horse many times before and had accomplished the mount. The boy leant forwards and snatched at the horse's reins confidently. Harvey readjusted the stirrups to the length of his short legs. His feet slipped neatly into the steel rings. He passed his fingers through the horse's mane.

'I love him. He is a great horse,' the boy said eagerly. He was keen to ride the course before the day's events to tell his friends.

'He shall win for us today, boy.' His father cupped at the horse's head and stared to his black eyes. 'We shall win today and this ride that we choose to partake in now will bring us luck on the course.' Taking a lead to the horse he manouvered it to the track.

'I want to go far. I want to go really far, as far as the farmhouse in the distance.' The boy pointed as he wobbled upon the saddle.

'Be careful,' Harvey demanded. 'Make sure that you concentrate. If you fall from a steed such as that you will be sure to hurt yourself.'

'I want to go racing, take me around the track really fast,' said the boy. He kicked excitedly at the sides of the horse. The horse scornfully, kept to a slow pace.

'Ensure that you hold tight, hold very tight,' said Harvey. His tweed trousers tucked at the knee to a chequered long sock that revealed brown wellington boot. He began to run. 'I will run with him and we shall ride you at a canter.'

The horse began to increase in pace, and as it did, the boy began to bounce upon the saddle.

'No. No. It is too high I want to be on my horsey it is much lower,' the boy stated with rising distress.

'You shall, my boy, just hold tightly to the reins and ensure your stirrups and we shall walk you around the course upon him and then you can spend the day with me.' The sound of the gravel crunching to the distance made Harvey turn, viewing a large vehicle that entered the forecourt.

The vehicle pulled beneath the awning that was suspended before the building. The foyer was accessed over a stair. A facade of glass provided views to a decorated interior that was filled with modern furniture. Harvey approached the vehicle with the small boy beside him. As the car became still, Harvey passed an angry look at Varman. Harvey chose to stand calmly before the large, four-wheeled drive.

'How was the boy on the track,' said Varman.

'I am not interested in a boy on the course, I want to know what happened last week,' Harvey replied aggressively. Varman removed his sunglasses and they stood a short distance from each other. A tall heavily built man with a full brawny torso, his lean face had bright blue eyes, and his head was covered with mousey blond hair. His tight-fitting trousers clung to his large legs and his jacket closed over a bright, white shirt.

'We need to speak about the way that you chose to undertake the command the previous week,' Harvey raised a short arm to point to him. Varman turned to face him.

'Harvey, relax.' Standing on the upper level he held his hands before him. 'I passed the command to the men, a group of associates that I know. They picked the kid responsible for the attack themselves. I did not undertake the task of choosing the boy personally. Leave it with me I will pay a boy that is reliable that will ride on his bicycle to the hut next week, and make sure they complete the task.'

'As long as you don't mess it up this time.'

'Today, you should relax and enjoy the gold cup, enjoy the races with your son,' said Varman viewing Harvey with caution. A chunky man with a rounded head and blazing eyes, he moved in an irritable and angry manner. (His tweed trousers tucked at the knee to a long, chequered sock.) Large gold rings adorned his fingers. Varman tried to judge how serious he was. Taking into consideration the large numbers of people present at the race day he felt reassured of his own safety. Should Harvey be angry at the failed incident then it would be spoken about when they were away from the racecourse. Harvey did not often tell a person until they were in private for a revenge beating.

'How did they miss him,' Harvey demanded. He viewed across the race entrance to a group of well-dressed girls. Waiting for them to pass he came closer to Varman. The small boy stood back.

'It was a simple task that was requested of you, he sits for the duration of the day in a small metal hut, there is little way that a mistake could be made. How did they miss him?' They walked to the entrance with Varman following behind, with each stride he felt upset. Harvey eventually lifted his arm before Varman to stop him.

'We can't miss him this time, don't worry too much.'

'Should you fail at your task through the week it will be felt that you are a problem and a sympathiser for the wrong,' Harvey said. Spittle stuck to his cheek and ear.

'You are spitting at me, Harvey. Calm down.' He touched his cheek with the back of his hand. 'It is a pleasant day, allow us to enjoy the racing together. I am able to assure you that the problem will become resolved through the week.' He gestured calmly. The small boy smiled.

'Spit. I am not spitting on you,' Harvey replied. He remembered a man that defied him. He looked the man in the eyes and with a deafening sound from his gun his eyes closed. The spray of blood passed up the wall. He collected the sports bag filled with money. Wiping the gun, he dropped it on top of the money and lifted the bag to his shoulder. He cleared his throat and spat at the dead man's forehead, it dribbled slowly down his face. They moved towards the entrance foyer that would allow them access to the race track beyond.

Reaching the entrance door to the box, Harvey with a shiny rounded face and furious rotund mouth, pointed towards Varman with his finger. Varman, staring straight ahead, listened.

'Should it become known that you know about what was a deliberate failed attack, you will become punished.'

'You should hold a little concern,' Varman said, calmingly to the man.

'A person is to be held at fault because there is visible damage to the interior rear wall of the empty cabin from a number of bullets. The cabin was empty and shots were fired,' said Harvey with fiery rounded eyes.

'They tried their hardest to get him,' Varman replied.

'The cabin is small and people are visible when standing inside it,' Harvey said angrily. 'We are not to be fooled. They didn't even try to hit the man.'

'I will make sure that the kid that is held responsible for the failed shooting is killed, how does that sound.' His lean face held a grimace and a furrowed brow. His lanky hard body stood tall and long.

'That is better. Make sure that happens and that the attack takes place next week.' He lifted his hand to point. 'No more mistakes.' The boy began to sob and he rested a hand on his head.

'It will take place, do not be concerned,' said Varman.

He thought of another job. The opening was too small. He pushed the man's behind and his clothes clawed against the concrete sides. They pulled him free. They each lifted a jack hammer and continued to open up the hole. They got him back into position, lifting him into the crevice. He crawled through the opening. They began loading their bags with trays of stones that began appearing. They shot the deceiver and left him there in the hole. He remembered the good times.

'Do you remember the jewellers,' Harvey said. His large rounded cheeks held a bitter grin revealing misaligned teeth.

'Yes, I remember the jewellers, it was a success,' said Varman smiling.

'We had small problems there that we overcame. You will do just fine next week, we can't let people get away with things.'

They stood before the large windows and viewed out to the jockeys taking mount on their horses within the enclosure below. They circled the enclosure and crowds gathered round to clap. At the starting line, horses were held by leads as they urged them into lane behind the stiles. The box was held with walnut panelling and a walnut counter ran alongside a wall full of bottles and glasses. Leather seats were arranged above a heavy carpet. Sitting in one of the leather seats, Harvey picked up a telephone. The boy sat beside him.

Chapter 2
Jerry

A soft rejuvenating breeze drifted through the terrace causing the trees to move their leaves and for the brightly coloured birds to squawk from high upon the treetops. They turned to view to them and the birds took flight to the clear sky with a span of colourful feathers from their bellowing wings.

'They are always here and perch in different places.' Amie's loud tone carried to him as they looked up to them. She leaned forwards and signalled with her hand for him to come closer. 'Listen Denem, you owe me for the contact, she is a tall brunette woman and you are not able to miss her.' She gestured away from herself with a hand, a heavy silver linked bracelet, on her wrist. 'So, you will be with her later on.'

'Yes, I should be.' Denem distracted, turned his attention to a group of girls moving slowly beside them with their bodies swaying to the music. He watched as their thin figures in tight cotton dresses moved at their hips to the music. A tall girl clutched a collection of shiny balloons by a long ribbon wrapped around her hand. The girls looked towards his face, at his green captivating eyes as he stood viewing them with his large sturdy pale hands at his side, a thin gold watch, revealed at the wrist of his fine shirt sleeve, shimmered in the sun.

'There are interesting people that visit here from the city later on in the evening, you will probably know some of them.' Amie viewed over her shoulder at the vast sparkling city lights before the high mountain peaks and turned, grasping in her hand a serviette that she touched with her fingertips and discarded to beside her.

'I am to find Stephanie, it is very important for everything that is planned that I speak with her today,' he said cheerfully to her over the music taking a departing stride from her again.

'A moment ago she was stood beside the gates with her friends, I could see her from here.' She rounded her hand to her mouth to shout to him through the music. 'Go and find her, she will be glad to see you.' She moved her hand to her pale bare chest to signal to herself.

'I am going to take the decision to search for her now.' Denem lifted his arm, his blue blazer sleeve held closed with gold buttons, and he pointed a long finger at Amie, standing tall and proud at her DJ stand.

'I wanted to be with you today.' She waved him away with a thin pale hand. Her face changed from serious to a large smirk, revealing lines on the pale skin of her cheeks.

'We will have lots of fun on a different day,' Denem hollered to her, turning to a group of slim women passing before them dressed in flowing silk dresses with short jackets across their shoulders and clutching leather wallets.

'Enjoy it with her and I hope to catch up with you later, you should try to finish up here with me at the end of the night.' Amie chuckling, moved her head with the breeze putting her hair to rest on her neck with the flat of her hand.

'I am able to view her, she is with a girl beside the entrance, at the timber gate.' Denem turned away from her to view across the crowded terrace in search of Stephanie. 'I wanted to stay with you but I am leaving with a feeling of anticipation for a planned new encounter, you understand I explained it to you, I have to consider the money and wealth that is likely to follow.' He watched people on the terrace collecting fleshy spit-roasted pig with glit dripping from beneath it onto plates. He touched the palms of his pale hands before moving one to rest on his belt, held with a horn brace piece above his tan trousers. Amie admired his brown hair, parted loosely to the side and catching the wind before passing her eyes across the heavy angular features of his face.

'You should stay here and drink these cocktails with me, they have got milk and cream in.' She pointed with her finger to a white carton of cocktail with a logo written across the side of it.

'They are bright white, are they tasty.' He looked towards her with his green beguiling eyes as she raised her glass with a star and writing branded across its front.

'They poured it from the carton there, they are good cocktails, don't go yet.' She stood before him grasping the White drink. 'Drink these with me.'

'We will speak more later this evening, Amie,' he cried delightfully to her, beaming through straight white teeth as he watched her turn from him in dismay with the eyes of her slim face widening as she began to make her music again from the records before her.

She pointed with both of her hands to him excitedly and began to raise her voice to him above the sound of the music. 'Stephanie has passed to the side of the pavilion, I can see her, go and get her quickly.'

'I am able to view her, she is a tall girl with brown hair speaking with her friend,' he said delightfully as he began striding from her and pointing with his hand towards her.

Amie stepped to the side of her music booth raising her hand to her mouth eagerly to shout, 'When you finish up speaking with her, be sure to return here.' She lifted her head proudly and her short black hair carried behind her with the breeze. He turned to view across his shoulder to her standing to the raised timber platform wearing a tight silver dress on her slim figure.

'I am leaving now, for sure. I'm going to find her, she is special to me.' Denem growled a tone that passed through the crowd raising his pale hand towards the sky to wave her off. A yellow balloon rolled across the ground before him.

She frowned her thin face. 'That is the thin little body that you want, just you look at it move.' She moved her flat hands and ran them seductively down the sides of her body over her tight dress. 'You can stay there with her all night and I will busy myself with others in future,' her defiant tone carried to him and he turned his broad body facing up to her, to reply. She leant forward, close to the edge of her stand chuckling and with a hand before her to steady herself against the timber dj box.

'I will return later on maybe,' he replied.

'You hold her, I am happy holding my records.' She lifted a black record with her hands, holding it high in front of her she spun it before placing the record down on the turntable before her. She smirked, opening her headset that she then released upon her head, she touched her hair to position it. He waited for a moment longer and then turned to walk away from her.

'We were here together before, a few years ago,' Denem hollered out loud to Amie. She stood up high with her record decks before her and with her hands held in front of her making her music.

'Yes, I remember you being here, you were at the event that followed with my friend, the drummer, she is coming here this evening and you will remember her when you see her.'

'The drummer's name is Carlie.' He looked upward to consider the girl for a moment, remembering her golden hair. 'I recall her, you both featured in a performance at my home through the summer and what a revelation that was to listen to.' Shells positioned on the steps caught his eye and he passed a smirk to Amie. 'It is likely that we will invite people to a garden party again this year and you could make music for us again from the terrace, there was a large number of us that evening and it seemed just right.'

She looked away from him as he spoke and viewed Stephanie and thought she appeared as her sister, she remembered her childhood. She began to consider her glamorous ill-tempered and rout sister, she threw items that she owned around her room recklessly. Amie would sit in her room, by a finely painted wallpaper of red roses in a dark mahogany framed chair with an embroidered yellow cushion depicting a small dog with a flat snout. She would clamber to her chair and position herself with her small legs before her, she would sit with her body straight backed to the padded rest with a glossy magazine, filled with musicians, across her legs. She was ten and she loved her sister, she would watch her standing, with her distinct figure clenching at her hands before her and stamping her feet on the floor beneath as she dressed, speaking impious and severe wishing for everyone less.

As Denem turned to stride further from the booth that Amie stood, a girl with a hairclip in the shape of a shell caught his attention as the shiny clip glimmered in the sun. He turned, viewing her fine cotton dress held tight to her chest but bellowing and flowing at her legs.

'Are you choosing to walk that way, I will speak with you as we walk,' Denem said to the passing girl that was walking in his direction. He turned his head to view Amie left behind.

'Walk with me but I am with a group of people over there.'

She simpered, and turned her head to gaze at him and then away to her friends.

'I know the DJ, are you enjoying the music?' He passed her a glancing look from his angular face through large green meaningful eyes.

She paused and then let out a small giggle to herself. 'There are a group of girls standing beside the pavilion rail, you should join us, another one of the girls that I am with says that she knows you through real estate, we saw you earlier.' She stood tall before him and passed her hand into the patterned fabric handbag held onto her frail wrist. Reaching inside she collected a bunch of keys with the keyring dangling from them between her long red nails. 'I am to collect an item from my car, go up there with friends and I will meet you when I return.' He viewed her broad face with high cheekbones and with brown hair in wisps across the soft skin of her face.

'I am searching for a friend that I know is here, her name is Stephanie and I am informed that she usually stands with a group of her friends over the other side there, so I am to find her there but thank you for the invite to join you.'

Denem viewing to the brunette girl beamed at her through straight white teeth.

'There you are, I thought you were hurrying to the car to get back with us and instead you are speaking with everybody.' A girl from behind her squealed and they both turned, viewing her approaching. Her friend, wearing a pink pleated skirt, waved her hand frantically at them beckoning them towards her. 'It is Denem I know him, it is so good to see you here.' She turned quickly to view her group standing at the rail, smirking from her shapely mouth before taking a step closer to his side. 'I am not often at the polo field and I did not know that you were visiting here today.' Turning to her friend she pointed to him. 'I know him from a club that I go to at the hotel.' Her blonde hair carried with the breeze and strands collected at her mouth that she removed with a fumble from her fingers.

'I am visiting the car, I parked and I am collecting a present for a friend that I left there,' she spoke to her friend, standing staring at Denem who had become distracted by commotion on the pitch. He viewed as a burnished horse lay on its side and kicked wildly as it offered it back legs, attempting to stand. They all turned and watched as the horse rose using its long twisting neck, lifting from its cumbersome struggling body whilst its lengthening jaw opened, revealing a foaming, screeching tongue. The people to the side of the horse viewed the sparkling sweating animal covered with sinew and muscle as its head lurched upwards in an attempt to climb, with its neck strained and curving, its shimmering wild eyes to the sky and with its nostrils flaring. From the head, tithes of hair created bundles and knotted strands that rolled across the turf of the pitch. The horse's blue saddle pad, lifted and fluttered with the breeze.

'I know the rider, we sit together occasionally at his stables.' He rested his hand on his thin belt touching a piece of horn on the buckle. They watched as the rider, wearing to the sewn figure twelve to his tight stripy cotton pullover lifted himself from his knees and stood beside the horse holding a polo hammer. Denem began to move towards the rider and with the blonde girl grasping his arm, he passed down the steps of the stand to the side of the pitch. As he approached the rider, the crowd parted allowing him a further view of the fallen horse.

'He can't get up.' He viewed the horse. 'He just can't get up, he took a fall and I managed to roll away. I don't know what they are going to do with him I just can't see him like this.' The rider standing with his hat under his arm turned away from the horse, and touching his forehead, began shaking his head. Taking a step away, his hammer fell to the floor and he lowered himself, crouching weakly bending at his knees to stare at the disturbed, upturned ground, beneath the horse. With his hands in front of him he began picking at strands from the turf, he twisted the grass with his fingers nervously before releasing it as he breathed deeply in search of composure as men gathered around the horse. 'I am not standing here for my horse to die, do something he is in pain.' He stood, and dropping his hands to his sides, he began to walk away, 'he has severed his leg.'

Denem raised his hand to his mouth to shout to him. 'Jerry you are now informed of events, and as to how they should be, as you stand there with dirty white trousers. It is a young horse that I wanted from you, a horse that you were offering nurturing and training to, it is only the beginning of your project and you were not with him for many years yet so there is not an excuse for keeping him.'

The wiry man with loose tumbling golden orange hair viewed him from blue eyes above white freckled cheeks shaking his head in disbelief, with a streak of drying flaking mud across the side of his slight face.

'Denem, I can't believe that he went down like that, he is finished, I am sure of it.'

Denem walked slowly to him touching the small man's shoulder, resting a hand and staring at him meaningfully through large green eyes.

'You will be fine, shame about the horse.' His large hand grasped to him as he leant inward to whisper in his ear. 'You will not allow that again, when you commit to a deal with me you should ensure it is delivered. I wanted that racehorse.'

The distracted rider, with his head down, turned and took a stride to return to the quietening, resting horse as it became submissive before them. A vet kneeled to the ground administering a large injection into his side. The horse lay still on the floor and the crowd began to move away, returning to the small stand and to the pavilion terrace. Choosing to sit on the terrace, Denem viewed a tall woman standing at the top of the pavilion steps beside his table set with a white table cloth with plates, glasses and yellow golden shiny salt and pepper holders. She stood admiring the riders upon their horses galloping to the far side of the pitch beyond the fallen horse. The girl intrigued Denem, and he viewed his solemn dark brown hair across his clothing to his blazer and to the shiny yellow shield held with crests of flying hawks, their feathered wings lifting high above their bodies.

'What makes a good moment?' he asked as he crossed his legs before himself, held with finely tailored trousers, on his body a shirt of crisp, white cotton.

'Fun and excitement makes a good moment,' she replied. He turnedm viewing beyond a gold number nine sign standing on the table, and reaching forwards he collected a large, frosted, white cocktail glass.

'We are making moments all the time, moments to remember.' He lifted the glass to the lips of his mouth before swallowing hard in pleasure.

Chapter 3
Stephanie

The stud farm had grey stone-built buildings holding the rich sleek silky chestnut steed that he had wanted to purchase. Now the owner stood before him, the pitch with his horse taken from him, he planned to reduce the wealth of the man further through business. He watched as spectators consoled him pitch-side, and as the horse trailer pulled away, allowing the match to continue. He wanted the steed from the farm and the man had promised that he would sell it to him, only to turn him away. He turned his head to view curly brown hair, resting sleekly on the slender back of the girl standing at the table's edge and replaced his glass on the table. This was the girl he was looking for and she had suddenly appeared.

'They are standing at the table's edge and aren't they fascinating,' Denem bellowed to the girl. She glanced at him from pale blue eyes.

'They are fascinating they are sure of that.' Her soft tone carried to him.

'You seem interesting we should take a walk together alongside the pitch,' he said confidently. The girl smirked with rounded cheeks rising on her face, she took her finger to her red lips, with a long nail, inquisitively tilting her head.

'You are quite a distance from me over this table, I may take a chair right beside you rather than walking.' Her piercing tone held. She grasped a flute of sparkling drink from above, and placed a serviette before him that held a star, stitched to the corner of the fabric.

'Leave whoever you are with, you are with me now for a moment.' She viewed Denem seated before her and lifting her hand began touching fingertips to his soft worsted blazer, held above his fine white shirt.

'You are welcome to sit with me for a moment.' He turned his head quickly, moving a small dawn moth that passed through the air before him, touching the patterned wings with the inside of his hand. He viewed her through enrapturing green eyes, gazing to her heavy brown loose hair falling in curls across her face. He viewed her distinct bony figure as she strode around the edge of the table.

'I will sit with you and we can talk.'

'Are you enjoying the game?'

'Yes, I am, now,' she replied. She wore a luxurious merino wool jacket wrapped around the lean structure of her body. AS jewelled fretted broach in the shape of a shell was proudly displayed to her lapel. She gazed at him expelling a soft eager breath before turning her head and with her thumb over her shoulder, pointed to a group of friends standing beside the pavilion wall.

'I am with people but you seem interesting.' She turned her head returning her eyes, that she held intriguingly upon him as her soft tone passed to him. 'Whilst I am standing here you may ask to me any question, ask it and if it is of worth, I will speak with you more.'

'What do you want to understand of me?' His egregious green eyes passed over her, from her ear across her neck to the lapel of her jacket, focusing to the bronze fretted broach with jewels and shells.

'Nothing.' Her thriving tone held defiant. 'I don't want to

understand anything about you, you can tell me your stories on other days.'

'You want for me to only understand yourself.' He raised both of his sturdy pale hands open before him and pushed at the air before him as if to push her away. 'Are you likely to know something that I do not know.' He smirked displaying straight white teeth and rested one hand to the white tablecloth. She paused with a frown at him from her long face.

'I am unsure as to what you mean. I have everything that I want and happiness, I do not require anything else from anybody.'

'Happiness. Do you think that is all that a person wants to feel?' He spoke to her reassuringly through his smile. She took a step closer to him, intrigued.

'You want to show me more. In that case we could plan to do something more together.' She sat on the chair carefully with her chin raised and her head held high. 'We may be able to make something more of our happiness that way and to make it last.' She viewed his angular face from her blue eyes and his heavy loose hair, parted solemnly to the side and enjoyed his appearance.

'Happiness always lasts when I am there, I make everybody smile if I want to,' he spoke defiantly through a smirk.

'Number sixty-eight on the pitch, take a look at him, he is about to score.' They both turned to view the polo riders as one collected the ball with his hammer and broke from the group. The crowd by the rail of the pitch cheered with waving hands and raised clenched fists.

'You are fun. I am enjoying sitting with you and speaking,' he hollered and brought his hand from his body to gesture to her.

'I find you intriguing.' She turned her head, viewing across the terrace locating her friends as she considered the fun that they might have together.

'They are finding happiness together.'

'I am feeling pretty happy, this day is turning out as I wanted it. It is good to meet new people,' her tone held him as she began pointing to him beaming from her face with thin pink lips.

'You are a find.' He viewed her pale smooth skin with lines either side of her shapely mouth. Her large rounded piercing blue eyes fluttered at him from deep within the frame of her face. He viewed her cheeks and nose as she lowered her long bony chin.

The humid evening air carried moths and their embellished wings whispered beside his face. He passed a large sturdy hand gracefully across himself to move them aside as he considered his new friend sitting before him. With a furrow his forehead he thought of her family and the many men that may be present in her life. She was of interest to him because of Dan, a boyfriend that she had had many years before. He wanted to conglomerate cargo from his factory with him. She would also aide in retrieving the precious script through contact with the many men that she knew.

'We should sit together for a moment and view the riders on the pitch,' he said reassuringly to her as he turned to view the horses on the pitch as loud spirited cheers carried from the crowd to them. She turned her head proudly away from him, the chin of her long face lifted high as she viewed towards the pitch. Her full distinct heavy dark brown hair rested beyond her shoulders in loose curls.

'We are meeting here today for the first time.' She gazed at him steadily. 'Do you find it unusual that we want to sit together right now, like this, it is so intimate,' her soft tone carried lightly to him upon the surging breeze passing across the terrace.

'We should take a walk alongside the pitch and view the riders and their horses.'

Her large rounded blue eyes cast over him and then the terrace of tables with the places set with white plates and yellow gold utensils with shiny spoons on a serving trolley. 'I promised a friend that I am to take a walk with her through the park and she is meeting with me in a moment beside the gate. We are visiting the forest to walk between the pools.' She stood up from the table and he stood slowly to join her. 'Did you visit there before?' she asked him. Her silk blouse bellowed before her in the wind as they walked from the table and she steadied it with her hand.

'I may join with you both beside the steaming pools,' he said as they passed through the final group of people before the park entrance and beside a snarling wire-haired terrier that revealed his jagged teeth from a tightly lipped mouth with dribbling foam. He could be heard through the scoffing and heckling of the crowd and they both turned to view him on the muddy ground.

'They are leaving this polo pitch with someone wild there.' She laughed.

'We will walk together that will be desirable for me,' he said as they both giggled with each other and she raised her hand and clenched his.

'They are sticking with them,' she replied, taking a few steps. 'We'll avoid the dog upon our return.'

A rider wearing a tight stripy pullover grasped a shiny metal lead by a leather strap that he pulled tightly with his arm to calm the baying dog before them. Standing at the fence the wearing turf around him held vacant from those passing that distanced themselves a step from the animal.

'I've got control of him guys, he will settle in a moment,' the owner shouted as he tugged at the dog, who began to lay before them. The large white animal bowed to the ground and began to wag his tail.

'We are content to keep our distance from you.' Their hands clenched together and his green eyes passed to meet with her own. He lifted his flat pale hand and guided her as he walked with her, gazing at the soft pale skin of her long face. He began considering the many women that he had chosen to share his time with through his life, to those that he had loved and wanted more and to those that he had chosen to forget. He considered those in his life that he had found partnership with and began to think that she may be more to him than just a way to secure contact with others to relieve the precious script. The script would allow him a secret code that would unlock a bank vault allowing him great wealth. Her beauty astounded him and he felt intrigued.

'Why do you think that we are able to speak with each other so easily upon meeting as we did,' she asked him softly.

'I find it easy to speak with people, I want to understand a person and to discover them.' He turned his head and his green beguiling eyes passed across her. She stared ahead doubtfully.

'What is it of my features that you want?' Gathering confidence she smirked from her thin lips, tilting her head to the side and viewing him.

'A person's facial features are to be distinct and familiar to me,' he said confidently.

'What else do you want from me?' She giggled gently knowing that her thin face was desirable.

'I want a person to yearn for me and for them to be lustful when provoked,' he spoke to her gently. She raised her elegant bony hand with her fingers bent and knuckles prominent holding it out in front of them for a moment before she began swiping at him with trimmed nails filed to a claw. She growled alluringly from beneath a gargling breath.

'As a person clawing at you for more, is that what you mean.'

He smirked pleasurably with his eyes held to the unsullied skin of her face.

'You are correct, they are to be wild and free.' His soft hands turned outwards from his side and he stared at her meaningfully. 'They are also revere me and to my tough body.' He viewed her and she took a step closer to him, her prominent frame covered with soft merino wool that he rested his hand on, touching at it gently along her forearms before resting his hands ontop of hers, their hands clenched together.

'I feel improved with you, I have got a grip of you.' She giggled quickly before stopping and taking a breath.

'I want to be with you as a friend, you are to partner along with us.' He grinned viewing down to her hands that were held with his.

'I am holding on to you, you are much preferred by my side.' Her soft tone carried to him, enjoying the way that they were speaking. She turned her head in search of Cathy, her friend. 'You are fun I like you. I will tell you. I should not say this really. I didn't dress for the polo, I am dressed for the walk that I planned to take with my friend. She is a dear friend and her name is Cathy, when I meet her you could join us if you wanted. I am eager to discover a little more about you.'

Her elegant hand rested on her chest, shyly, with her long fingers curled to her bare skin as she viewed his angular face and his brown hair brushed solemnly to the side. Tilting her head to the side, she considered to him as a person. She wanted to trust him, but it was just too soon. She always trusted men too quickly she thought.

'We will walk together now.' He gazed at her.

'I want to understand a little more of you also.'

Hearing him, she confidently lifted her chin and her brown shining hair fell loosely in splendid curls across her back and the bony cage of her long face. As they walked, he turned his head to view those admiring her around them, many people gazed to her as she strode with vigour from sturdy legs confidently past groups of people walking towards the polo pavillion.

'You remind me of my younger years, there was a person like you.' She raised her hand tapping him with the back of it, on his shoulder. 'There was a place that we would go to many years ago, a club.' She smirked from her frail lips with her eyes held on him. 'A club in the city that I know, we would sit with many friends and men would pass beside me and I got to know this one guy quite closely. He was from a family close to ours and he reminds me of you, he had the same features and mannerisms as you.' She moved her hand beside her face pointing to her own features with a circle of her finger.

'Tell me of the club,' said Denem. He thought of the digital script and considered to those that she knew at the club, perhaps one of those men would help him take possession of the script.

'I always sat to the same table when I visited and that was my favourite table. It was a room that I adored, with deep red ochre walls and a high ceiling.' Becoming excited she took her long thin hands out flat in front of her to describe it. 'The rooms were always interesting with bull horns attached to the walls.'

'What else, tell me more,' Denem hollered to her. She remembered her evenings, sitting comfortably on the embroidered cushions of the club with cocktails sitting before her, and her friend. They would choose brightly coloured cocktails with sugar glistening on the rims of the martini glasses from a choice of a long list of drinks. She would collect with her long hands the flaring glass, taking sips of the liquid to rest on her tongue whilst taking sly glimpses through bright blue eyes to the mutedly lit room across the outlines of wealthy men in discussion. She leaned her bony body closer to Denem resting her hand to the soft cotton of his jacket sleeve. 'I am to meet my friend and then we could enjoy martinis together later on, perhaps.' She grinned at him through fragile pink lips revealing straight teeth.

'That sounds like a very good idea, we could enjoy the club together if you liked.'

'I want to go for a drink at the club with you.' She pointed at him with a long elegant finger.

'We will go one night. I am interested in meeting with your friends.' He viewed to her through green eyes.

'We are going to the club, how exciting,' she said as he turned his head to her with a smirk. 'When we meet with Julia, the friend that I was telling you of, you are to speak to her of our meeting. I cannot believe that I became drawn to a person as quickly as I did.' He watched as she strode, with an elegant hand passing to her side.

'I will happily speak with her, I am quite excited that we are all meeting,' said Denem.

'I really enjoyed speaking with you today and I will say, I really like the way you dress,' she spoke excitedly turning to view his blazer and finely tailored trousers.

'I dressed for the occasion.' He viewed her up and down and enjoyed how they both appeared together. She considered clothes when she was younger, with her sister. Her sister was older than her and when they dressed together, they talked about clothes.

She had wispy curly hair, a lighter brown than hers. It fell across her shoulders resting on the soft cotton of the shirts that she would wear. Their distinct pale faces were both bony and long with large round eyes, deep to the frames of their face and with high cheekbones, joyous indentations passed to the sides of their mouths. She would sit with her long limbs folded beneath her on her large oak bed with carved posts, clutching her elegant bony hands to her ornate ivory handled mirror, collecting tissues from a dispenser to touch up make-up, as she applied it to her eyes. Stephanie would choose to sit, turning the pages of her sister's glossy magazines with pictures of thin gaunt women held in sombre pose. She would consider whether she would be like her sister as she grew up and whether she would be like the girls to the magazine. She was shy and bashful with people throughout her younger years, nimble and diligent through her schooling. Her family were wealthy and affluent, from generations of prosperity and she had grown to an assured and alluring woman, with a group of well-mannered friends.

Chapter 4
Julia

She stood beside a furore of steaming water that spread out across the rocks. They began to reach to the ground to collect sticks, clutching a bundle in her hand, Julia threw them into the boiling water that bubbled within the dark openings within the jagged rock. High grass grew lush and verdant beside them and scaled lizards spread across the crevices of the rocks covered with a blanket of green moss. The two girls took a step closer, staring down at the openings in the rock together grasping each other's hands, gently . Stephanie, loosening from her grasp, collected her handbag from her arm and gathered a pink leather wallet in her hands revealing a shiny address card for the club.

'This is the address card for the club that I told you about, we could head there later on this evening.' He took the shiny card from her.

'When you meet somone like you, you have to consider whether that person can be enlightened or whether they enlighten you,' Denem said to her as he approached them.

'You have to be enlightened by people otherwise it just becomes arrogance.' Widening her eyes, she viewed his dark brown solemn hair in the warm breeze and his blazer with glistening gold trim on the lapel.

'I will make you aware and uplift you with knowledge,' he said softly.

'I am excited by that.' She lowered her chin as she gazed towards him. 'We are going to the club together, that is for sure, then you can tell me plenty more.'

'They are going to the club, it should be a good night.' He chose to stand beside Stephanie and to watch as Julia chased the sticks in the pools with her eyes.

'It's exciting and fun with them, they are together as a three.' Her silken tone passed to him. She raised her bony elegant hand flat before herself, and stepping from him, she suggested her favourite companion was Julia.

'We are all together,' Julia shouted loudly over the sound of the gushing water.

'We are together later also if you want to come with us to the club, Julia.' He viewed her brown curly hair, shining splendidly in the warm sun. Stephanie's eyes focused before her with a blink from long lashes and she passed a graceful bony hand moving frolicking moths fluttering at their patterned wings before them.

'What do you think of my new friend?' Her intimate tone carried to him. He widened his green eyes gazing over her shoulder.

'When you speak with her more you will enjoy her.' She turned her head, lowering to her noble chin to him shyly. Her arms swung to her side and her fine elegant hands were open beside her. He reached forwards with his fingertips, touching her long face, beside smile lines on her mouth. Julia stood tall, with a light green cotton dress on her body, held with thin straps on her shoulders and her legs lengthy and pale, staring into the black pool with prominent cheekbones and blonde hair to her shoulders.

'Come and watch the sticks swirling in the pool, you see your reflection when the pools are still.'

'When I view down into the pools, I am able to see something very beautiful in appearance.'

He howled a tone that carried as he approached Julia with Stephanie at his side.

'This girl right here is better looking.' Julia looked down at her dress and then peered at the pool. She turned her head to the side, proudly raising to her chin and viewing him defiantly.

'We are a fun group and we are much better together,' Denem replied. Stephanie viewed her friend before them, and walking to be beside her, with her long bony arms moved evening dusk moths from her face. They surrounded her with their tiny abdomens supporting stippled fluttering wings.

'The pools are always good to look at.' Standing beside her friend, crouching with her hands to her bare knees, Stephanie's slender figure came close to him before she leant her elegant bony hand to rest above his shoulder touching to the soft, worsted material of his blazer. He viewed her through mesmerising green eyes touching her back.

She stood close, whispering to his ear, 'We are together beside the pools for sometime, shall we return to the pavilion?' She peered over his shoulder, towards the pavilion building that stood brightly lit surrounded with flickering lamps.

'Who are you sitting with?'

'There were two tables of friends that I sat with earlier and we could join to them again when we return. One of the tables is a group that we ski with, we hardly ever see each other unless we are on the slopes and they are here for someone's celebration.'

'I will join you at the table, there are many that say that sitting with me is a dream.' Julia's sad tone carried as she gazed at Denem through pale blue eyes.

'Why would they say that sitting with you is a dream, I do not understand why they would say that.' Stephanie, frowning, spoke to her over her shoulder noticing her attention on him.

'If you are a dream then you are a vision, something only imaginary,' said Denem questioning her.

'I am unobtainable to some people,' Julia answered carefully, taking her arms to her hips to stand defiantly. 'Not everybody gets me.'

'You are wonderful and desirable, my dear friend, now come along with us.' said Stephanie. She began to think of the men she had met through her childhood and those that she had lost. She remembered a waiter lighting candles on a smoothly iced cake with icing animals and the occasion with her family at one of their residences. An elegant man with an angular face and heavy dark hair passed beside her to speak with her sister, older than her, she was more accustomed to men. Her splendid curly hair was a lighter chestnut than her own. She was more defiant than her and would allow nothing to pass should she not like a person. She had slowly and sensuously turned her young pale lengthy face with her eyes shyly lowered upon him. Initially, she had not recognised him and those surrounding her did not say who he was. From a young age, she had met with many popular people that she was familiar, the older members of her family had contact with the most influential throughout the country. The man, visiting from a different family, had been invited there by her father and she had been ignored because of her sister. She turned her blue eyes meaningfully to Denem, she had learnt her lesson. If this man was important then she wanted to know him and she did not want to lose this opportunity.

'There is a moth on you and you are likely to want to remove it.' She reached out with her hand to move the moth from his shoulder and it fell to the floor crawling across the turf.

'Are you OK, Julia? You don't mind me being with you both, I know that you usually walk alone.' Denem said to her. He lifted his graceful hands with flared fingers to in front and he pointed to her.

'It's pleasant to have you here with us both, I like you. They get a smile for that.' She beamed through thin lips. Stephanie, watching her speak, lifted a graceful hand with fingertips to touch his heavy, loose, brown hair on the back of his head. Julia viewed her in her red merino wool jacket with a large gold broach pinned to the lapel, and with an elegant stride from her thin pale legs, linked her friend's arm. She collected her close, embracing her, and softly touching the wool of her jacket to her skin to feel the warmth.

'I meet with many people, Stephanie, but you are by far my favourite.' Julia's tone passed to her with mild guilt at her beginning to seduce him.

'I know I feel the same. I was looking for you in the pavilion earlier, I thought you were with a gentleman then. He is all mine if he continues to be pleasant like this,' as she spoke, she moved slowly from him and moved her long face close to the blonde hair of her friend.

Julia smirking, stepped forward removing her arm from the her friend's she faced Denem, her hand to her side above her flowing green pleated cotton dress with a button stitched to the shoulder.

'We are meeting for the first time, what do you want to know about me, everybody wants to know something.' Her woeful tone passed to him. He took his eyes across her bare chest revealed to him by the curved low neck of her dress passing his eyes down to the edge of the fabric.

'What do you want to change,' he passed a tone that held to her. He watched Julia's blonde hair carry in the wind over her credulous face.

'We could sit and discover change.' She smirked through lips laden with lipstick.

'We are deciding to discover change together then but who will guide, I believe that it will be me in allowing you an understanding of yourself.'

'I might want that.' Her thin hand moved from open before her to rest at her side above pale legs with canvas shoes tied high around her ankle.

'I am content with our arrangement here, are you both?' Stephanie took her hands to her hips and furrowed her brow with a glance across her shoulder.

'Always contented meeting others.' Julia's tone held sprightly as she lifted her head to her with wide angelic eyes, which looked meaningfully at her friend.

'What do you like of new people?' He spoke confidently standing between them. 'Speak of what you hope to find with them.'

'Deviance, I want them to be naughty and to tease me.' Her tone passed blissfully to him. She lifted her hand to touch her shining blonde hair into place.

'You want for an understanding of yourself from what I know.' He viewed to her hair against her pale skin. Feeling an urge, he prevented himself from lifting his hand to touch her, because of Stephanie beside him.

'Are you able to arouse that from me with what you know.' Her sombre tone carried to him.

'We should find out.' Denem replied.

Stephanie, viewing to them both, moved to Denem, and taking his arm, pulled herself to him enjoying to the soft worsted of his blazer as it touched her elegant hand.

'That's enough you two, I'm with him first, Julia,' said

Stephanie. 'She has first choice with him.' She frowned at Julia as she pulled him closer.

'They are far more beautiful, aren't you, Stephanie. She is very important.' Julia looked to him with a smirk from lipstick covered lips.

'They are getting him, this girl stays where she is standing right now.' Her tone blossomed outwardly.

She took a direct gaze at his eyes, he simpered. 'Who are you?' She took a step closer to him and her feet flattened the leaves. He beat them to the floor as he grasped her with urgency with his large, steady hands grasping her hips as she took her limbs to steady to her figure. Her brown curly hair cascaded and tumbled behind her as she struggled gracefully to steady herself.

'I am for you.' Her tone thrived heavy and acclaimed with excitement. He inhaled air through his nose and they kissed with a touch to their lips, she dropped her head shyly and blushed from her large eyes. She looked to him longingly as he lifted his large hand to touch her hair, moving it from her forehead to the side of her temple. She took herself close to him again, and relaxing her limbs, she rested her head on his shoulder. He moved his head towards hers and his straight nose and face to her hair. She gazed up to him longingly, before slowly pulling away from him. 'How do you think that you will get to know me more, you have to do more than kiss me.'

'I will ask you things, so that I can understand who you are, your good and bad points, allowing me to understand you,' he replied.

'Good points only with me.' Her tone flowered and her blue eyes widened. Staring before her, she raised a dignified hand to touch the collar of his fine white shirt, revealing from above his blue blazer. He viewed her hand and then, in longing, to the pale skin of her face, held the resting curls of brown hair.

'You want to understand both from a question for it to mean something, to make you remember it and for it to mean something that you will hold on to,' he spoke as he turned his head from her to view the tall trees with silver bark, at the edge of the forest beside the pavilion. She touched the angular features of his face and admired to his broad jaw.

'What are you two doing, I saw that affection.' Julia's weeping tone distracted them as she took a few steps beside them, with her hand on her thigh catching her dress bellowing outwards in the wind. 'You and him are close friends now and very quickly. I hope that you are right, Stephanie.' She began to walk from them, sullenly.

'They make all the right choices for themselves,' Stephanie's tone thrived to her.

'We are the closest of friends, you shouldn't worry, I'm not selfish. Just as long as you are happy,' said Julia quickly.

'Your friend is always there for you, that is good to know,' Denem cried with rapture, viewing them both. The large silver tree trunks of the fir trees beside them held a dark canopy of black needles and cones, covered the ground.

'It is becoming late and the light is fading.' Julia raised her wishful tone over her shoulder to her friend.

'Did you stop and view the pools for long, there were large toads,' he asked a tone to her.

'We saw them.' Stephanie took a smirk from her distinct pale face. 'Denem, we had to be careful not to plummet into the water when we were crossing between the pools over the large rocks.' She moved her elegant hand to her long brown curly hair to settle it from the breeze. 'They bubble also.'

'Some of them bubble and there are cooler pools with lilies,' said Denem.

Stephanie raised her elbow out for him to link to her, and with her other arm, pointed upwards with a tilt to her head to view the knotted branches and twisted leaves of the tree canopy above.

'Where will you take me, Denem?' At her flourishing tone Denem viewed her long pale face beaming with straight teeth through red thin lips.

'I want to go somewhere with you very soon, we are to make plans.'

'Wherever you want to go, someone right there will take you,' he bellowed with delight.

'Partnered with them there, we'll most certainly go together.' Stephanie's voice blossomed as she past a glance to Julia.

'Friends like that don't get left behind, where will they go?' Julia pinched at a curl of blonde hair with her fingertips leaving it to place on her cheek.

'What shall we plan for now?' Stephanie strode with thin limbs close to him, she touched the open palm of her bony hand to her jacket sleeve to remove debris from the park floor.

'We could visit the fairground tomorrow,' Denem said passing his blissful green eyes at her with a stare. He lifted to his hand to remove some debris from the weave of Stephanie's red merino wool jacket. She tilted her head and her hair fell forwards in brown curls.

'I agree there is a fairground wheel to the lakes, a friend was there talking about it, it has views to the park and we should ride it.' Stephanie raised her elbow and slender arm upwards, and with a fine hand, pointed to a large tree beside them covered with red leaves.

'We will go there if you want and view the falling leaves

from that tree. It is maple tree, it is different to the trees surrounding it. Try to catch one of the leaves in your hands for me.' With an eager tone and without waiting, Stephanie excitedly bounded with large strides to beneath the tree of falling leaves. 'Look at all of the different shades of red and orange on these falling leaves.'

As Stephanie walked away from them both gazing towards the trees, Julia released a hat from her hand, it caught the wind and was blown, falling to rest upon the floor amongst broken sticks and crisp fallen leaves. Denem bent to his knees to collect the hat with a grasp from a large hand. He viewed the green hat with a feather held to its side by a leather strap. Julia, understanding that her friend was distracted by the trees, collected the hat from him with a swing to her hips touching his soft hands and with a flutter to her eyelashes.

'You like him also, Julia,' said Stephanie, surprised, with furrows to the forehead of her face.

'I am going for the leaves also, I do not want him, you were kissing him.' She spoke touching her blonde hair calmly with her fingertips. Stephanie turned away from her, and ignoring her, took large strides past them both grasping a floating red maple leaf. She let out a giggle.

'There are plenty of leaves to grasp hold of,' Julia yelled to her as her pale hands grasped outwards to the sky at the cluster of leaves clutching them between her fingers.

'With a catch, they are held tightly in my hands,' said Stephanie smirking to her friend before turning to Denem.

'They are all together catching leaves, what fun.' Denem linked his arm to hers and she became close to him, viewing the angular features of his face and his graceful dark brown hair, parted to the side.

'I'm excited with the thought of fairground rides.' Stephanie's tone peaked. She chuckled and Julia turned to them both. Taking a red maple leaf held at the stalk, she presented it to the sky.

'The leaf that you caught to your hands,' Denem cried loudly. She held the maple leaf in front of him. 'Bring it closer, show it to me.'

'Why is that of interest when you are able to look at me?' she asked him in a flourishing tone pointing at her finger to herself.

'The interest is held because you caught it and want to show it to me,' he said standing with a deep blue blazer open at the buttons and his white shirt to his belt and over his fine cotton trouser. 'Explain what you like about it.'

She considered him with a tilt to her head and then followed with a smirk from fine white teeth through pink lips.

'I enjoy the veins that run through it, they are intricate and run to a pattern.' She laid the leaf flat on the palm of her large, open hand.

'That is sweet,' Denem said.

'No, syrup is sweet. maple syrup.' She pushed at him with her slender bony shoulder gaining his attention. He looked at her from his beguiling green eyes. She viewed his face with a broad jawline and to his heavy, loose, brown hair, ruffled and parted to the side, catching to the wind.

'Ice cream syrup is sweeter,' he said. She released the leaf from her elegant hand to the ground and it floated, resting on the rubble and sticks laying above the park floor.

'I know, we could go and eat sundaes. — I know a great place.'

Chapter 5
Denem

Beside him in the cabin of the car, she viewed his face and his broad jawline, she reached out to touch his thick hair and he turned, viewing her seriously through large green eyes. His sturdy hands rested on the leather steering wheel. Before them was a gated gravel driveway. They viewed the building in the distance, its tall windows framed with fine leading and glass panes that shimmered upon the approach. Red slender brick buttresses faced the vehicle and the roof was covered in deep grey slate. The entrance was an ageing oak door positioned within a heavy stone fluted surround. A reef of twisting green leaves held the face of the door and rustled lightly in the breeze. The door opened as they approached and a young man, wearing a smart black suit with a tie and a white shirt, stepped forward to help him with his suitcase.

Denem turned to view from a window across the sprawling glistening city beyond with small white houses across a landscape filled with crops and cattle beneath a wide clear blue sky. He viewed the buildings in the distance considering the work that he had undertaken as an investor in the city. He viewed the distant shiny towers standing clustered high above the city, many of which he was responsible for building, and to the houses on the valley floor. They reminded him of being a small, young boy in one of those houses, he would work with his father crafting furniture. He would sit beside a small fountain and often lean to touch his hands in the water, watching his own reflection. Large clams with hoary husks rested in the base of the reservoir. White and cream fish swirled to the depths of the water, passing over each other's scaly bodies. He would balance his nimble body on the sturdy marble basin collecting water from a protruding spout. A worn inscription of a family name was on the wall. He would watch his father completing the gleaming cabinets, the layers of polish revealing his hazy outline to the dark doors.

'Do you visit your father often?' Denem said with a furrow to his brow. 'I am not always able to collect you from there and I do not wish for lengthy discussions with him.' The two of them sat in the stationary car before the large red house. Denem released his door and she viewed him across the cabin as he stood and began to walk towards the view. He wore a blue jacket and a fine white cotton shirt with tight trousers.

'You enjoy speaking with my father, he is always interesting to visit and speak with,' Stephanie shouted through the open door excitedly, taking her soft black handbag by the strap and collecting a compact from inside. She viewed her reflection and then closed the bag.

'It is his friends that are interesting, if he is with the families that I expect him to be.'

'Let's enjoy being together today. I will help you with script not him. I think the guys at the club have it. Dan will know who has it.' She frowned at him. 'Where are you going with me Denem, today, we were planning to be all alone together.' She smirked and exulting lines appeared on the cheeks of her long pale face, her heavy hair resting forward across her shoulders. He viewed her brown hair taking the soft gentle breeze from the hillside.

'Look at that view there,' he said. 'That is a beautiful view.'

'We are going to that room.' She pointed with her hand to

the red brick building stippled with shade from the surrounding trees.

'Come on let's go.' She began to walk away, excitedly turning to see if he was beside her and beckoning him with her hand. They laughed loudly together and she nestled beside him grasping his arm. She touched his soft cotton jacket over a white shirt. She smirked from straight white teeth through thin pink lips. Denem raised a large open hand blissfully sheltering the sun from his eyes.

'You are able to enjoy views back across the city from here, I often forget.'

'I don't want to understand the city, I want to understand you. Take me to the room.' She touched her hair with the fingertips of her elegant hands to settle it from the wind.

'Enjoy the view, Stephanie, for a moment. If you look there.' He pointed a finger to the distant houses. 'We passed those large built blocks on the journey here and the ground floor on the street are filled with people.'

'How many blocks do you own?' she said.

'We don't own them all, we sell them or sometimes people live in them and pay us rent.'

'I am curious about something,' she chortled. 'There are unique little shops at the base of some of the buildings that you own and we should walk around them another day.' Her brown hair fell to the sides of her pale face in loose curls. 'Do you own them also.'

'If we own the block we will own the shops, I like to choose the people that own the shops and to understand what they are selling. Aston says that I shouldn't care. He is business minded, a great aide.' He turned his head to her, his dark hair passed the angular features of his face.

'When we climbed the hill in the car to arrive here, do you remember that from the side window we were able to view the large houses, they were adorable I want one to live in.'

She pointed a long finger towards the houses. She touched her hand to the sleeve of his soft, blue jacket. 'I want one,' she demanded with a stamp of her foot.

'I have many friends that reside in the property in that area of the city,' he said excitedly. 'There are houses crawling to the southern side of the hills on the rocky slopes, all of them offering views across the hillside and to the distant valley.' Denem stepped forward with a graceful stride, and with one of his hands swinging to his side, he considered the gift of beaded jewels that he had arranged to be delivered to the room for her. He glanced at her through green eyes, and she lowered to her chin shyly.

'I purchased a gift for you that I arrranged for you to collect from here.'

'It will be in the room,' she said. She clenched her hands together before herself in excitement.

'Shall we go inside.'

'I want to go to that room up there, Denem.' Stephanie pointed at a window to the hotel and viewed the garden landscape. 'There are magnificent views from that room across the manicured gardens.' They walked together across the noisy gravel. Peacocks stood proudly in the drive with their silver and blue tail feathers displayed behind them. The stone walls of the building were covered with blue budding flowers and climbing greenery.

'The room is always the same room that I take,' Denem said. 'From the window, a river runs through the valley.' The wind passed across his face and he grasped his jacket, buttoning it. His green eyes were surrounded with fine warm lines from his smirk.

'We will sit in the window and view the river.'

'We'll enjoy doing that together,' she said. Together they passed the large oak entry doors embellished with twisting vines, petals and leaves before striding over the pure white marble floor of the entrance hall.

He passed across the busy hall, standing with Stephanie before a large window. With the fingertips of her hand, she began to pull the soft silk scarf from her neck collecting it loosely in her elegant hands, her bright blue eyes rested upon him. She threaded the silk item between her long graceful fingers.

'Do you see this scarf that I am holding?' She took it taut between her hands before him. 'I want to wrap it around you for fun.' Patterned sofas and chairs, with embroidered flowers were positioned above the heavy weave carpet.

'Bring it here to me now to touch the fabric,' he ordered, taking the fingertips of his sturdy pale hands to the soft shiny orange silk. 'Where were you when you chose this?' His green eyes passed to her.

'We were at a house in the countryside with friends and it was a gift.'

He lifted his large blissful hands before him and she wrapped the scarf around them.

'Do you make friends closer to you with a gift, or do you purchase a gift because you are close already?' he asked.

'A gift brings us closer to people,' she answered with her blue eyes settling upon him.

'You will enjoy the gift that I have for you to the room then,' he replied.

'The scarf is in my hands and I have four long limbs for you to wrap it around.' She pranced with a look over her shoulder to a sofa, her soft hair ruffled with splendour behind her.

'Take their gift and wrap it around me to secure me close to you.' He grinned. She stood before him in a white merino wool jacket that he touched with the back of his hand. He turned and viewed a group of girls in the entrance hall.

'Shall we visit and speak with them,' Stephanie uttered.

'I think we should remain here for a moment.' She bent to sit on a sofa and he nudged at her with his hip and she fell upon it.

'I am always honest with you,' she said. 'You know that.' She touched his leg.

'I am truthful and full of honour,' he replied settling into the seat beside her.

'I am truthful too.' She beamed.

'That honesty keeps us strong, we are falling in love with each other.' He rested his arm on the cushions with a smirk. She gave a flustered chuckle, repositioning herself on the chair, before collecting a cushion from beside her, to hit him with.

'Take that,' she said as she struck him.

'Stop hitting me with the soft cushions or I will get you later on.' As the cushion pushed against him, a grey and black feather passed in the air that she blew with pursed lips.

Chapter 6
Jamie

He viewed her distinct tall bony frame standing with long limbs and low shoes upon the white marble floor. She tilted her chin and her splendid brown curly hair fell across her long pale face. She became distracted by the window and he looked at shells embroidered into the seats and it reminded him of his father's paper shells that he would make from origami. He remembered as a boy, his father taking paper in his ageing dry hands and he would fold the corners to a sharp crisp point. He would view his hands and then up to his face, and his bright green egregious eyes surrounded with wrinkles as his father concentrated on the paper in front of him. His father guided him and taught him. He folded the edges of the paper and unravelled the small folded sheet an intricate white shell. He would drop the shell into his small cupped hands. He would practice replicating the shells with his father viewing him, he was supportive and directed him. Leaning forwards, he took a sheet of paper from before them and folded a shell, that he dropped it on top of the pad.

'Look at the park from that window, the opening in the forest is where we were standing when we met,' her tone flourished.

'We met at the polo pavilion, you are not able to see it. It is behind the trees over there,' he smirked through straight teeth. 'We were listening to the music and the polo match was in view.' The window offered views across the park through fine leading with a centre piece of intricate yellow flowers. Beyond the park, rows of tall green fir trees grew deep before the mountain peaks.

'That is where we were standing, at the opening in those trees,' she said. She became excited and straightened the spine of her back above her seat. 'I'm able to see the place that we kissed beside the polo club.' She quickly turned her body, elated, and collected her hands in a grasp on Denem's arm.

'That was a special moment,' she said. He viewed a large group of women in the lobby. A tall woman with mousey-brown hair, wearing a pleated dress with heels, moved to stand beside Stephanie.

'They are a group that I know, shall we go and speak with them?' She turned her head of heavy brown hair.

'Speak with them and I will sit here in the chair, beside the fire,' he said. Stephanie gave a small shrug of her shoulders.

'Jamie, it is you.' Her loud squeal carried and she raised her hand to the group. 'I can't believe that you are here, it is so good to see you.' She pointed to her friend as a waiter collected a glass before her.

'We are going to the restaurant.' The blonde girl smirked from rounded cheeks on her oval face.

'I wish to speak with you, it has been so long,' Stephanie said.

'Tell us all about your new friend,' Jamie asked gazing towards Denem.

'You have not met him yet, his name is Denem and we have been together a while. I met him at the polo club beside the park one afternoon.'

'You should bring him here and introduce him to us,' Jamie said suggestively.

The girls in the group sat in the lobby chairs, with their fine clutch bags at their sides.

'He is an investor,' Stephanie said provocatively. She stood wearing a soft cotton jacket with a white silk shirt and tailored trousers.

'Go and get him over here, I want to speak with him.' She was reminded of her modelling days, sitting with her leather-bound planner. Tall thin models dressed in loose flowing trousers and high shoes passed her desk, with waves from long hands. She sat in the lobby as a secretary. A finely dressed ageing man with glasses and a tightly rolled silk scarf on his frail neck visited her desk, and leaning to her he grasped the telephone from her hand. Lifting his glasses to his forehead, he ordered her to stand, ordering her from around the desk. He asked her to pirouette in the lobby. She took a deep breath, and collecting her shoulders back, she focused in front of her and began to stride. She was in the wrong place at the reception desk. He took her from the desk and gave her a career.

'We could go over there and speak with my group of friends if you wanted, you did not speak with them before,' she said. Denem sat wearing a blue jacket over a fine white cotton shirt. 'You are looking great today,' she said with a chortle.

'Come and speak to my two friends.' They passed across the marble floor to the two tall girls. Jamie, with mousey-brown hair, turned to view them. Stephanie raised a hand to touch the arm of her new friend, Denem. 'What do you think of him.' With large captivating green eyes he viewed to the girls.

The two girls stood up from the lobby chairs and strode across the lobby floor. Tall white ceramic pots with large blue crests to their fronts held leafy trees with pink flowering magnolia.

'We are going to eat now will. Bring your new friend.' Jamie viewed her friend's long pale face and Denem standing tall beside them. He lifted a sturdy hand before him, a thin gold watch glimpsed from his sleeve.

'We are to eat, we'll group together for the walk to the dining hall,' Denem said.

'Stephanie, I am so glad that you are here,' Jamie replied. They walked with the group through oak doors to the dining hall. They passed an oak panelled hallway with pictures in golden frames. They entered the restaurant and Stephanie turned to touch his soft jacket, taking him close to her as they viewed the dimly lit room. High windows on the walls, and the room's oak beams, had a motif.

'The room that we have chosen is filled with bronze-framed lanterns,' he said. He raised a finger to point to a distant side room alight with flickering candles and lanterns.

'View the décor of the dining hall, it feels morbid in here.' She viewed the dark green room. 'I am glad that we are to sit in a side room to enjoy each other's company alone,' she said. He passed his green eyes to view her ahead of him, her splendid curly brown hair on her slender back. Together they passed her group of friends who took a table in the dining hall.

'We are passing that room there, it looks beautiful,' she said, as she pointed to the door.

'We have got our own privacy in this room.' He viewed the pale skin of her face.

'Love makes us want to be with each other,' she said viewing the bronze lanterns swaying.

'When we are with each other we build love,' he replied, searching for a seat in the small room.

'I could be with you always,' she said.

'We should be together continuously, I think of you all the time.' He gazed at her.

'The room is amazing, Denem, it is hand-painted wallpaper,'

she said. They sat at a large oak table with lit candles. The walls were covered with intricate hand-painted wallpaper of climbing verdure and entwined leaves. bronze lanterns hung on the walls.

'There are gold embellishments,' he said, raising an open hand to direct her to the wallpaper.

'The leaves and flowers are whirling in a pattern that I enjoy. I want something that is finely painted for your home, we should ask a person to visit.' Stephanie touched the wallpaper with the tips of her bony fingers. 'Denem, let's sit at the window together, the view is amazing,' she spoke excitedly, striding towards it.

'The table is very large,' he said as she walked to the table running the fingertips of her hand on the finely crafted oak. Denem went to the window with her, and they viewed the mountains.

'Take a seat close to me instead of sitting a distance from me.' She touched her hand on a chair beside her. She turned to him and slid her pink crocodile skin wallet across the table. She began touching his brown hair with her fingertips.

'The wallet bag was a gift from my father, he knows the owner of the fashion house,' she said.

'That is interesting, did they make the bag for you?' he replied.

'Our family shares ownership with them and they enjoyed it, as they made it. I adore it,' she said gazing to the bag.

'It is a fun wallet,' he said. Seated with his long legs crossed before him and his hands resting above the soft cotton of his trousers, he turned his attention to the waiter.

Chapter 7
Dan

He seated himself in a fine walnut chair with a soft cushion behind him. His large hands rested on the arms of the chair. His long legs in a fine cotton trousers crossed before him.

'There is a moment of enjoyment in meeting with another person, what makes that enjoyment lasting,' he hollered, his large, fascinating green eyes on her.

'There is bliss in meeting anybody if you care enough about them,' Stephanie said attentively.

'When you discover someone new that feeling of enjoyment does sometimes fade quite quickly.' She touched his dark brown hair. 'They do not always hold the same understanding that you do of things.'

'We are understanding together.' He chuckled. 'I like it that way.'

'The room that we are seated in, is beautiful, Denem, I am glad that we met today.' Stephanie's eyes gleamed bright blue. She touched her ear revealing a white pearl. 'It is not my first time with you here.' The room surrounded them with Walnut panelling and a heavy weave carpet.

'Open the door, and we will enjoy the music together.' A piano played in the large hall beyond the room. He felt happy with her beside him, they were becoming increasingly close. The large doors opened and music filled the room.

'The music is vibrant and lively.' Her soft hair ruffled by her face. 'I like his manner, when it builds to a crescendo.' She gazed at Denem. Circular shells were on a bowl on the ledge of a curved alcove.

'He wants to stand as he makes the music, he is used to larger venues,' Denem said with his long legs crossed.

Stephanie sat before him with pale smooth skin. The structure of her pale face held with heavy cheekbones.

'There is a casino we could visit. It is to the side of the hotel, a short walk across the courtyard,' she said. Her lips turned upwards with a smirk.

'We will visit the tables,' he said. 'Together we will go in front of the others with wins.'

'I enjoy roulette. I always win,' she said. 'There are a group of girls that I meet with occasionally and we began to visit a casino beside a hotel in their city for fun.'

'We could go there together, we will visit your friends.' His angular face revealed white teeth. 'How do you choose to position yourself in the game?'

He viewed through egregious green eyes to the distant white statuette of a bust.

'I have got lucky numbers for my game, numbers that I recommend to a person,' she said. 'We could begin by eating at the restaurant at the hotel, they serve a suckling pink pig that I adore, and then visit the roulette tables with money.' She viewed him reassuringly.

'A baby pig. The finest tasting pig are fed with acorns.'

'The baby pig is succulent there, they roast it for hours and it arrives with small horns.' She collected her fingers to make two little horns above her curly brown hair. He laughed. 'Red or black, I always win.' She pointed to him.

'We will be sure to win with you.'

'You will enjoy one of the pairs that I know, her male friend holds at investments.' She lifted her hand to a heavy crystal glass. 'He is an investor like you.'

'We could all visit the casino together,' Denem said excitedly.

'It is intimate and the room is lavishly decorated.' With her hand she lifted bread to her mouth for a bite. She took the bread with a pull from her large white front teeth.

'You are a rabbit,' he said. 'You appear as a rabbit with those teeth.' Her long pale face chewed at the bread.

'Don't you go on.' She took the stem of her glass between finger tips. 'You are a rabbit.' She smirked. 'You are commenting on my front two teeth, you should look at your own teeth.' She gave him a stare. 'I know what you are getting at, you are suggesting a look of madness.'

'They are mad funny, they look like a rabbit,' he said. Widening her eyes, she made a crazy look at him, tilting her head to the side.

'Enough with the rabbit,' she murmured.

'We always make something funny of the occassion, I like being with you.' He clenched his teeth to a smile. She furrowed her brow.

'Are you choosing to drink the wine also, my mind is feeling the effect.' She could feel her body tingle. 'I always choose this wine, it is twelve on the list.'

'There is not a requirement to forbear and refrain ever but it does show control of self,' he said. Her curly hair took a sheen from the candle.

'It is a change of focus that allows abstinence,' she said.

'I believe it to be self-control.' He stared at the glass. He touched his hand on the napkin across his legs. She moved her hand to her warm forehead. The door to the room lay open, allowing them to listen to the pianist.

'I am becoming used to your accent.' He moved strands of hair from her face. 'Tell me more about the place that you were born.' He gazed to her. She enjoyed his tenderness.

'We will speak about me more if you like.' She blew her hair to move it from her brow. She chuckled. 'I lived in the lakes.' She became doubtful for a moment and gulped from her drying throat as memories flooded back to her.

'You are thinking of the place that you lived or the people that you spent time with?' he asked.

'There was a person that I knew and we would often meet at the lakes. We lived together. I thought about him for a moment there, he was of interest to me,' she said.

'When you visit again where will you go, will you visit the place that your friend lived,' Denem said.

'I will go beside the lakes, where we have a residence.' She became abrupt with him. 'I am thinking of a friend, a guy called Dan. We used to be close.'

'Tell me more about him,' he enquired.

'I like the lake and the boats, but I want it with somebody different now. He is forgotten.' She thought about Dan and wondered if visiting with a different person, such as Denem, would aide in removing any longing. She stared at the window thinking about Dan and how close they became. 'Our family owns the house and I still visit there.' The table was set with places on a white tablecloth. She began to lose herself in her past.

'Tell me more about Dan,' he said.

'Dan, my friend, visited me here, and we lived together, now he has purchased clubs in a number of cities.' She pushed backwards from the table.

'He was a close friend of yours, you should make contact

with him again.' He wanted to meet Dan, and although he was growing fond of her, he had to remind himself of the real reason behind them meeting at the polo pitch. He wanted the script.

'We were close.' She became sad. 'I do not want to think about him any more, we will visit to the lakes alone, Denem.' She looked at him with still blue eyes.

'We will go to the lakes together.' He pointed to her cheerfully.

'He was a dear friend but you are my friend now.'

'Where is Dan now, which city?' he asked. She looked at his angular face.

'He sits in his club.' Her rounded blue eyes half closed in thought. 'He owns them all, there are so many,' she squealed. 'Why are you asking about Dan so much, let's forget him we are eating together. I do not want to be reminded of him any more.'

'We were speaking about friends, I held an interest in him that was all. Relax a little,' he said trying to calm her.

'Over with it.' She smirked through white teeth. 'What do you do when you are away from here, let's speak about you.' She lifted her elegant hand upon his.

'I focus upon my investments.' He collected his wine with a sturdy hand. 'I am busy throughout the country.'

'When you visit the country again, we'll go everywhere together,' she said.

'Yes, we will enjoy the country together,' Denem replied.

Chapter 8
Jamie

Stephanie grasped a flute of sparkling drink on the table with her long elegant fingers. Denem released a button on his slim jacket, and with a pinch to his trousers, became seated.

'Take more of that if you are enjoying it.' He gestured with a large open hand to the tray. She leant forwards seductively, hitching at her skirt.

'It tastes good I will drink plenty of that,' she said, her curly brown hair falling across her cheeks.

'I need to ask you something, it means a lot to me,' he said.

'You can ask me anything, you know that,' she replied, touching to her hair.

'I want you to meet with a group that I know and to build relations with them, allowing business that I am undertaking to conclude.' He pointed to her with a large hand. 'I will pay you for the meetings.'

'I would rather not, I am busy,' she replied.

'It may be necessary that you enter into relations with one or two of them,' he said. 'It's for business.'

'No, Denem. I cannot believe that you are asking me this, I will not do that I am with you.' She frowned. 'Why would you want to think about arranging meetings for me like this, I thought that you liked me,' she said. She opened her legs, revealing her bare thighs. She chuckled. 'I only want you.' She looked at the flames in the fireplace.

'It may be necessary that you spend time with these people

and stay with them for a short period whilst we are still in a relationship.' He rested both hands on the arms of the chair. 'You are to do this, and that is that,' he said. He collected a flute of sparkling wine.

'I am not sure,' she said.

'There is a club owner that you know, we spoke of him before, I want you to reacquaint with him. You knew him many years ago and I want you to begin contact with him again for me,' he replied.

'Who do you mean, not Dan, surely,' she said shocked. Denem viewed her legs as she seductively walked away from him. 'I'll not be speaking with Dan, I did not speak to him for many years.' She touched her thin lips with her fingertips. 'We were close, we had a relationship many years ago I told you this, I do not wish to see him again now.' She became sad.

'He is important to my business operations and I will pay you,' he said. He crossed his legs before him.

'I like you, Denem, you know that I do not like him any more, I knew him many years ago.' She stared at him seriously, moving a strand of hair from her face. 'Is it really necessary that I see him.' She became angry and began to gaze out of the window. 'My life has changed since we met in the park, Denem, and I enjoy being here with you. I want to see more of you not him.' She reached out to touch him. He looked at her.

'We will remain together, but you are to do this for me,' he said seriously.

'I am not sure, Denem.' She stood from her chair and he watched as she crossed the room to stand before a window, she rested her body in the window seat.

'You will be paid, and if you do not do it, we will not stay together, it is only for a short period,' he said.

'I will do it if I have to, but I am with you, not him,' she replied. She didn't want to lose him, she had not been happier since the meeting in the park. They had enjoyed so much together.

'Visit him on a number of occasions and then say to him that you know me and we will all become close, I wish to understand those that surround him and the group that he is acquainted with. He has a script for a bank vault that I want.' He furrowed his forehead.

'I will do it for you, Denem.' She touched the small ivory buttons of his shirt. 'Jamie is visiting here this evening,' she said.

There was a knock at the door, and Jamie entered and placed her soft, tan, emu-skin wallet on the heavily cut oak table. She stood with her hand on her hip, wearing a bodice, and bangles at her wrist. She passed him a sly wink from an eye with long lashes. She moved her long fingers to the table, to signal a choice of drink.

'They are cool, they have got crushed ice in their cocktails,' Jamie said. She passed her eyes to Denem and then to a bucket of ice.

'Yes, there is crushed ice,' said Stephanie.

'You called us to the house and now we want to know all about you,' Jamie said.

'I met with Denem at the polo pavilion I told you earlier, he is an investor.' Stephanie's heavy long brown curly hair tumbled onto her face.

'I work as a model and I am returning from an important show today,' Jamie replied. She sat on the seat, slumbering forward comfortably with her elbows. She passed a distant hazy stare at Denem from her light blue eyes. 'I take to the catwalk for fun.'

'She thinks that she is more beautiful than her dear friend,' she said.

'I will interrupt this bout, take a seat with me.' Denem directed them to the table.

'These friends of mine, they are lucky fto have your company,' she whispered in his ear, her hand touched lightly on the soft weave of his jacket. Jamie, watching them, rolled her eyes, happy for them.

'I want to know what you have to say, tell us something.' Jamie said softly.

'If I was to say that there is a deep blue sea with waves cresting high and white that carries to the far distance, and ask what do you want from it, what would be your response,' he said. His large green eyes followed Stephanie, and he smirked at her.

'I want to be seated upon a large boat, on soft cream leather, eating and drinking, passing through the waves,' Jamie said.

'A boat with all of us on it,' said Stephanie.

'You could take the ocean and visit islands, and visit them on your boat.' He turned to Stephanie. 'Islands in the sea.'

'They could have shops on, anything that you needed,' said Jamie. She began tapping a silver ring on the table, excitedly. 'Clothes shops, lots of them.'

'We have got to take a boat some place at some point,' said Stephanie.

'Yes, we'll all go together,' said Denem.

Jamie collected an olive with a stick. He viewed her through green eyes.

'Tell us about Aston,' she asked.

'He works for me.' He took a hand to beckon to Stephanie. She moved closer to him. He had chosen not to discuss Aston with her, through habit, he had always kept his business separate.

'I met him through Dora, his wife, we've known each other since childhood.' He sat back to his walnut chair.

'If you want, we will travel and visit her, Denem,' Stephanie said. 'I am beginning to understand your life and the people that you are close to.'

'You are suggesting visiting a friend that you know,' said Jamie. 'What part of the country are they living in?'

'We often meet at their residence, it is a large country house,' he said.

'We were speaking of our return from travels abroad with the models, Stephanie, it was an arduous trip with them all.' Jamie revealed her legs, and a patent-heeled shoe.

'How many models are there now, Jamie, at your agency?' Stephanie asked with a seductive tone.

'There are many,' Jamie said. 'Listen, before we speak about them, it was suggested on the telephone that we were getting the new company. I forgot I am excited.' She began clapping her hands. Stephanie returned the gesture, patting her hands also.

'On our visit, we began talks for a company takeover with some guy that we are held to contact with for the last year.' Jamie sat back in her chair.

Cathy remembered her younger years when she would stand watching her mother working the manikin taking cuts of material and wrapping them around the plastic torso balanced upon their small kitchen table. A tall woman with curly hair and large round blue eyes, her thin body lumbered over her work. She would stand beside her passing her measurements. She stooped over rolls of material cutting precisely with black handled metal scissors, the lavish material held with chalk lines and pinned with thin crunching tracing paper stencils. She would work the order book for her mother, passing the various measurements for her to work. She monitored the orders for the supplies and the addresses that the articles of clothing would become dispatched to. The large log with a stiff leather cover she would keep neatly in the cupboard beside the shiny enamelled sewing machine with bobbins. Jamie returned her sultry lazy gaze to Denem.

'I may take one of the small pots,' said Jamie.

'It is just sugar and fruit, it is made from ripe strawberries with the ice.' Stephanie held up one of the glass pots.

'Frozen ice, I like it coarse,' Denem said.

'It is made through a churner, to have it coarse they scrape at large chunks of ice,' she said, with short blonde hair at the sides of her head. 'Now you know.'

'Frozen ice,' Denem said. 'We'll eat plenty of that.' Cathy rolled her blue eyes.

Stephanie tapped at one of the pots with her spoon. 'If you add milk, it becomes sherbet.' She touched his arm. Cathy scooped at the red ice.

'Everybody knows that if the ice is coarse, it is granita,' Stephanie said.

'Give me a strawberry pot,' Denem said. He took the strawberry sorbet pot in his hand, and passed a grin at the table.

Chapter 9
Ryan

The finely painted roses and flowers covered the enamelled roof of the arcade, held above by thin fluted cast iron frames. The curved glass windows were filled with weaves of wool over crafted cane furniture and held to a line above black polished veined stone. Standing in front of the butcher's shop, he took the view up to rigid partridges with a shimmering plumage of feathers. white tiles covered the walls. A hog with leathered skin hung on a hook. His white eyes rolled deep inside his head. The door opened to allow him a view of the butcher. His weighty torso beneath a clean blue apron. He bent forwards and rooted with a the metal trays of piled red meat.

'The poultry you have up high in the window looks very good quality.' He viewed a basket of fruit, collecting a fleshy apple in his hand. The sleeve of his shirt revealing a timepiece. 'I viewed the sign for the shop as I passed beside the arcade. I am shopping today.'

The butcher's hands rested awkwardly on his lumpy hips. Taking a deep breath his chest raised proudly.

'You see before you the finest.' He raised his arms before him. 'This is the very best produce, from the farms on the hillside.' He viewed Denem standing in tight brown trousers and a coarse heavy weave brown jacket. The butcher grasped a yellow pencil and struck a line in his neat figures held on a sheet of paper. 'That is an important man standing there.' He prodded his soft chest with a thumb.

'They are important enough to be here buying your goods.' Denem replied gazing from him to a row of guinea fowl.

'We have it all, please take the choice,' he said. 'You are able to get what you want from here,' he spoke, looking to a tray of birds.

'Could you speak with me further regarding the sourcing of your meat.' He viewed the butcher's ponderous wrinkled skin.

'Yes, I will, sir, the meat has been sourced from a number of local dairy farms with cattle in their fields, many of which are located high up on the hillside and are visible through that window.' He pointed to the window.

'They have got luscious creamy milk that I collect too,' Denem said. 'There are a lot of cows to that hillside.'

'You are able to see them before you to the height of that hillside, the meat is collected from there to here.' He placed down the sharpener onto the metal countertop. He turned to look at churning enamelled machinery. Shiny metallic bladed spindles ground with troughs filled with white animal fat.

'They have got the very best,' Denem said. The butcher's stomach pushed forward from beneath his apron.

'We know what we have got and that is some of the best produce.' He returned to face him through serious rounded blue eyes.

'I've got plenty to choose from,' Denem said.

'We have the very best selection of meat for you, why don't you consider one of these.' He lurched forwards and collected a cut of red meat, holding it before him. It passed limply through his fingertips.

'Dark marbled beef from a fine cut of the cow.' Denem glanced across his shoulder to the window to cows standing in the distant landscape.

'You cannot beat a good cut of steak, sir. We have a selection.' The butcher swung his wide brawny arm above the counter. He stared seriously through rounded light blue eyes to Denem. He stepped forwards and pointed to a barrel of fillet steak.

'That steak is of quality, it is deep in colour and has heavy marbling across the face of it. I'll take that.'

Denem watched as a lank faced boy with abundant mousey hair stepped doubtfully from the doorway, his fingers covered with minced meat. He moved beside an oak block on which a balding cold rigid bird lay, he put it into position at the neck with a mire covered knife.

'I listened as you spoke from the room.' His brow raised from his feeble face. 'You are unable to beat a chateaubriand, sir, they are from those cows.' He pointed to the window.

'It is a cut of meat that should be shared.'

'It collects the nutrients, sir, from the intestines that is why it tastes so fine.' The silver-haired butcher smirked.

'The chateaubriand also strengthens the animals' spine,' said the boy. The butcher gazed at the hillside.

'Take him a piece from the counter to show him our good cut, it is a grainy flat piece of meat.' He looked at the window crossing his hefty bare arms.

'A good choice of meat held there,' he said.

'Somebody, tell me something interesting, it's boring in here all day.' The boy's feeble body straightened and he pointed to Denem.

'You are enjoying yourself boy,' the butcher gazed at him. He purveyed the shop with his stomach protruding. 'Weigh a piece of meat for him.'

The boy grasping the brown, grainy meat, lifted it to the

waxed paper on the scales. He gazed at the counter.

The spindly faced boy cast his deep russet eyes across the work surface to the cutting block. He lifted a metal handled clever cutting beneath the rigid partridge's shimmering flecked wings. Denem rested a hand from a heavy weave brown cotton jacket to the package of wax paper held on the counter.

'There you go, take that.' He raised a tense hand with fingers spread his mousey hair.

'We will enjoy some of that this evening.' He gave a naive grin.

'Thank you, young man,' he said to the boy.

'He is above me and did you know that he trusts me to prepare all of this meat for him on some days before he arrives the shop.' He dropped the cutter.

'Ignore him, sir, I am here in the side room changing into my apron and hat whilst Ryan begins to prepare,' he said. He searched for his missing hat before pointing to the straw boater on the window sill.

'There is always a day that you are late for various reasons and I have the work done before you arrive.' The boy leaned on the side of the cutting block.

'Trust is lacking, sir.' The butcher crossed his arms over his fleshy corpulent stomach.

'If you are able to trust, there is good in a person.' Denem focused upon him.

'Why would you want to trust anybody when people do not trust each other,' the gaunt boy replied.

'Trust is obvious if there is good in a person.' His green eyes rested upon his frail body.

'Why would you ever want trust when there is doubt, they are not always good when you meet with them,' said the boy.

'It is for an understanding of others or we do not meet people.' Denem's assertive tone carried him. A loud bang passed from the arcade as a weighty slate chalkboard with a sturdy bronze frame scraped against the shop front as it carried in the wind. Denem turned to the door. 'The chalkboard has fallen with the wind.'

The boy on his tiptoes viewed over the counter and through the door.

'In addition to that fine cut of beef, we should also discuss the other choices that we have in the shop,' said the butcher.

Denem strode before the curved counter his sturdy legs in tight brown trousers, and a warm beige shirt with a belt, with a coarse heavy weave brown jacket. Denem turned, resting a pale hand on the counter. Spruced purple meat with a side of trimmed wide glutinous fat held flimsily on protruding grainy bones, spiny racks of lamb leaned on each other revealing scored patterned gristle.

'What would you suggest?'

'You are viewing the lamb. I enjoy it with herbs, I baste it for a long time before cooking it slowly.' His high tone carried with eagerness.

'That is good advice I will consider it,' he replied with a grin. 'Collect me a leg.'

Ryan revealed a tally of fawn teeth as he lifted the lamb on the palm of his hand.

'These legs are heavy.' He nimbly removed a sheet of blue shiny waxed paper and flipped the lamb onto it.

'Enough of this, take the leg of lamb to the low counter,' said the butcher. 'We will have it for us to both look at there.' He looked at the boy who shrugged his lean shoulders.

'Pass to me the small meat knife,' he said. They viewed the

flatly cut load of splendid gleaming flesh.

'Here take it.' He took the meat knife with a snatch and pointed towards the meat.

'The leg is cut from the sheep with a saw that is positioned high inside the groin before removal. It is then pulled outwards releasing it from the cartilage. We then tendon saw the meat to release at the flesh.' He banged the knife down on the counter. 'I just wanted you to understand our work.'

'That is fine I understand, thank you for telling me,' said Denem.

Denem passed beneath the row of hanging birds with their drained rough orange claws held to ceiling hooks.

'You do not visit here enough, when you are shopping visit here. There are other regulars that visit our shop,' said the boy.

Denem looked at the boy's stained shirt, and blood smeared on the bare skin of his inner forearm.

'I am shopping here today and I plan to venture further along the street,' said Denem.

'We know everybody around here and they all come in here.' Returning to the flat of his feet the boy began reviving to the meat before him.

'Is the boy your son, is that why he is working with you?' Denem said to the butcher.

'We are a close family. My daughter is a lawyer. She took her tests and there were not many in the whole area that achieved what she did that year,' he replied.

'It is good to understand a family,' said Denem, smirking at the boy.

'I was always aware of her abilities, she lives far from here and is a great success through her work.'

'What about the young boy standing beside you, his abilities are good also. Look at him cut that meat.' Denem lifted a hand, pointing a finger at him.

'Come and collect this, I am wrapping it for you.' He stopped and placed his hand to above the bird.

'Do you want the pheasant also.' The boy pointed to the stiff bird laying across the block.

'Yes, I do, I want the pheasant. Take it to the bag,' Denem replied.

'Before you continue with your shopping journey, you should consider these.' The butcher pointed to a tray of balding fleshy birds.

'I will grab you a bird,' the boy said. 'There is plenty of choice for you there.' He grasped a bird in the palm of his hand. Gripping it firmly, he placed it on the counter with a thud.

'A rabbit,' the butcher demanded. 'A rabbit, dear sir. That is what I am asking, if you want.' He began to make a sucking sound with his tongue in his dry mouth. 'A dry palate if you fail to prepare it correctly.' He then revealed his front two teeth above his bottom lip like a rabbit. The men turned their heads astutely, staring at each other.

'You are like a rabbit with those teeth,' Denem said. He collected his meat from the countertop and began to leave the shop, heading down the arcade to the street where he planned to purchase a newspaper.

'I am similar in appearance to that of a rabbit but I am not filled with madness like those that are viewed at the roadside with myxomatosis,' the butcher said, pointing to a furry pelt of silver rabbit.

'You are referencing a person taking psychotic medicine, they are rabbits,' Denem said. 'A person on pills often appears rabbit-like with a dry palate and large front teeth visible.'

'Enjoy your produce, sir,' said the butcher. 'Don't shop too much.'

'I will enjoy the produce. Which way is the newsagents, I want a newspaper?' The butcher and the boy both raised a hand and pointed down the street. A young woman with blonde hair entered. She looked at Denem, with a longing gaze.

Chapter 10
Issy

The woman stood to before the shopfront wore a red coat with a white ribbed cashmere sweater that pulled tight across her chest. She handled magazines from the rack before her, flicking through the pages with her hands glancing at the advertisements.

'I always purchase my magazines from here,' she said resting her camera on her hip.

'We could purchase magazines or have them delivered,' he replied.

'I always shop for my magazines and then I catch up on the frontpages of the newspapers.' Denem lifted his arm, his blue blazer sleeve held closed with gold buttons, and he pointed a finger to the stand.

'That is one way of shopping,' he said.

'We are always without something unless we browse magazines for the things that we want,' she replied. 'I always have my goods delivered.'

'Chocolates deliver,' he said, gazing beyond her to the window before them filled with chocolate figurines. She looked at the window of the shopfront beside her filled with chocolate ballerinas that stood on stands, spinning. He moved a step to stand beside her and together they viewed the reflection of themselves in the glass. A short girl with natural mousey brown hair with a small face and a snout nose. Her lush plump cheeks framed untamed dark eyes.

'What is your name?' he asked.

'It is Issy, I do not often shop here, but the jewellers was broken into and I am reporting on it.' She lifted her camera. 'That is why I have got my camera with me.'

'What happened at the jewellers,' he said.

'They dug a large hole beneath the building and burrowed their way into the riches,' she replied thoughtfully.

'Will you be taking photographs with your camera?' He raised his hands to gesture to her camera.

'I will be taking photographs for the local newspapers and if the photographs are good then we will sell them to the mainstream newspapers also,' she said.

'That sounds terrible, I wonder who it was?' he replied.

'It was the burly city boys.' She touched her hair in the reflection.

'They are a rough group of lads,' he said.

'A man died,' she replied, surprised. A man with a wide face and a grin opened the curtains to peer from inside the shop. He had a rounded cut of hair and his face filled them with warmth.

'Come inside,' he called to them. He began pointing at the chocolate ballerinas. Issy made her way to the shop, and together they pushed at the large bronze door handle. Brightly coloured ballerinas wearing dresses finely piped on their bodies stood on racks. Denem aided her collecting her magazines. Issy placed her bags on the floor. The bag before her toppled over and her reels of film rolled to the floor. She peered at him with uncertainty as he collected the items in his hands. They gazed at each other and she fluttered her eyelashes.

'Thank you for collecting those items for me,' she said as she stood from crouching, gazing at him. Her figure was short and slim. 'What a good beginning to my day, I want for nothing other than to be with new people like you that help.'

'People find it difficult to help others.' He viewed a ballerina beside him.

'Show me the style of clothing that you find the most interesting to the magazines,' he said. She collected the magazine to her side and began flicking at the pages.

'There is an advertisement that I want to show you.' She raised the magazine to show models entwined. She laid the magazine across the counter and her bright suede skirt lifted to reveal her thin legs. She pointed to the page.

'I enjoy the richness of the textures that can be found here in this photograph.'

'You sound as though you know about the subject,' he said. He gazed at the picture on the page of the glossy magazine.

'Look at some more with me,' she said.

'Let's take a look at the chocolate ballerinas instead.' He pointed to the chocolate ballerinas that filled the shop. They stood on the worktops covered with silver wrapping paper. The ballerinas held a pose with their legs above them as they pirouetted on a small podium.

'What are these over here?' she said.

'They are petits four, shall we sample at them.' He moved to a display of petits four that were upon the glass screen of the counter. He stood beside her in a finely tailored coat. Denem looked at her and she collected a coated chocolate from a display between her fingertips.

'They are delightful, why don't you try another one?' she said.

'I will enjoy one more with you,' he replied.

'What do you want from a person,' she said gazing at him.

'You have to understand what makes a person special to you,' he said.

'What makes me special to you.' She collected her camera to her side.

'It is everything about you,' he said.

'You can be special without being in love, dear friends are special,' she replied thoughtfully.

'If you care for me and I care for you then that makes you more than special,' he said. She giggled.

'The taste is delightful,' Issy said as they continued to choose from the chocolate display.

'What about these over here?' Denem stood viewing to a girl wearing a small pink dress. She ran towards him in the shop with a chocolate lollipop. She pointed to a man in a stripy apron and braces holding a large usherette tray.

'We have got lollipops for all of you,' he chanted.

'He has many chocolate bars,' said Denem. 'Shall we help ourselves to some.'

'We could take a few,' she said.

'How do you decide what is beautiful?' he said.

'It is what is keen to your eyes. It is what a person deems as beautiful,' she replied.

'Am I keen to your eyes?' Her small mouth had full red lips her nose was short and snub. Wild wispy brown hair covered her forehead.

'I have only just met you, but you seem beautiful inside,' he said.

A tall woman clutching the handles of two large bags filled with chocolate boxes began to leave the shop. She brushed past them as she left. Issy collected her camera to her hands, and turning to Denem, she clicked at the shutter.

'I will take photographs of you, to remember you.'

'That is one way of remembering a person, I will remember your dark eyes and brown wispy hair.'

'I will remember the way we spoke,' she said.

'That's nice,' he replied, smiling.

'I always use my camera for my reporting.' She touched it with her hand. She remembered reporting upon a large crash. A number of lorries had tipped over carrying flowers, and boxes had covered the road. Other cars had cascaded into the boxes and veered into the central barrier, catching fire. People trapped inside their vehicles had become burnt. She had visited the scene to capture the crash on her camera and to report to the local newspaper.

'How am I looking on film?' he said.

'Let me take one more of you,' she replied.

'I will move to the display of figurines and you can capture them also.' She snapped another photograph of him.

'No more photographs in here please,' said the shop assistant. A tall shop assistant with fair hair stood before the counter waving a finger. He moved to the till. The shop assistant completed the packing of a tray of chocolate truffles. Denem glanced at a glass cabinet filled with figurines, before collecting in his hand, a chocolate rabbit that he took to the countertop beside the till. He took a card from a silver holder and passed it to the reader.

'Is that all that you want,' said the cashier.

'Yes, that should be all.' He looked at the assistant through green eyes. He passed him a smirk. The assistant tore the receipt and placed it in a book with a staple before dropping it from between his thumb and forefinger to his bag. Denem grasped hold of the handle of the small shopping bag and lifted the bag from the countertop.

'What is your number,' she said, leaning towards Denem. He passed her a business card and smirked. He lifted the bag that held the figurine up with his hand. He left the shop with her walking beside him and they set off along the street.

Chapter 11
Varman

The factory building was grey with large glass shiny windows along its side. A tall grey chimney stack spewed smoke from the side of the building. Large doors opened wide to allow deliveries. Inside Varman unloaded boxes from a series of vans.

'Varman you are delayed in arriving, you were to meet with me this morning, you are to ensure my protection,' said a squat man with a rounded head and large fiery rounded eyes. His loose suit hung from his body and the arms flapped around over his wrists.

'What is wrong,' said Varman, concerned.

'I expected you to collect me in the car from the house and I was waiting for you,' Harvey replied, getting angry.

'Relax, what are you worrying about. You are more than able to look after yourself,' said Varman, taking a step back.

'You are to collect me and be my protection. You did not arrive at the house.' Harvey walked over to him and put a short stubby arm around him.

'You know where I was, I was with her,' said Varman looking down at him. A tall heavily built man with a full brawny torso, his lean face had bright blue eyes and his head was covered with mousey blond hair.

'I was waiting for you at my house for most of the morning,' said Harvey.

'I chose to stay at her home through the evening,' Varman replied.

'You could have woken early and collected me, it wasn't necessary that you remained in bed with her,' said Harvey.

'I do not see her very often and I found it difficult to leave, she goes on at me,' Varman said. He was concerned that Harvey might become violent.

'I require your protection so in future when you are planning to collect me then make sure that you do.' Harvey banged a roll of film hard onto the work surface. Varman began collecting boxes from the back of the van putting them onto the ground. Harvey steadied each box. They then cut away the wrappers with large craft blades releasing the separate packages.

'We should make smaller boxes from the pre-folded cardboard to stack the items into,' said Harvey.

'I will make the boxes,' said Varman. He had several boxes stacked before him that he placed the unpackaged machinery into.

'Close the boxes and lift them into a smaller van to the rear of the unit,' said Harvey. Varman began closing and sticking the boxes with machinery inside.

'The boxes are ready for loading they are all stuck down,' he said after several minutes.

'A number of the larger boxes should be kept whole and should remain on the lorry to be collected as one consignment,' said Harvey.

'I will make sure that happens,' said Varman.

'I want to check the count and to split a package from the centre of the consignment,' he said.

'What boxes do you require,' said Varman, concerned.

'I require the boxes from the centre of the consignment,' said Harvey angrily.

'They are located on the van still.' Varman a tall heavily built man, continued to push at a large box to position it before turning to Harvey to shout over the noise of the engine.

'Take the boxes from the van and begin to open them,' said Harvey.

'There is a problem with one of the boxes, it appears to have been damaged during transit.' Varman shouted. 'Could you please take the time to come and take a look.'

'It has become damaged during transportation,' said Harvey.

'Show me the location it was positioned in the van,' Harvey replied.

The men climbed aboard, and choosing to take a number steps into the back of the van, he pointed towards the deck of the van at the position that the box had stood. Harvey bent his body forwards to study the damage to the box. He crouched to look at the box on the deck of the van to source the problem. Small diamonds were spilling from the box onto the floor.

'I cannot imagine that any heat from the motor or exhaust of the van would pass into the cabin. I would suggest that the package became damaged during transit,' said Varman, standing in the lorry and staring at Harvey. Harvey stood over the split package upon the floor.

'The package has the diamonds that I ordered.'

'Take the diamonds from the box, I shall contact the supplier,' said Harvey. He looked at Varman. They lifted the box, with Harvey scooping the diamonds that had released into his pockets.

'I will carry the box inside,' said Varman.

'The box is filled with diamonds,' Harvey whispered.

'We will unpackage the box here.' Varman released the box onto the work surface and they began to steadily release the diamonds into a tray.

'Take the diamonds and put them aside,' said Harvey.

'What are we doing with the machinery beside them?' Varman's lanky hard body stood tall and long. His jacket was buttoned at the front, covering a crisp white shirt and tough body.

'We will repackage the machinery.' Harvey collected the diamonds with his fingers. 'This deserves a reward.'

'A reward?' said Varman.

'We will go upstairs and enjoy a whisky, because we found the diamonds,' Harvey replied.

'Let's go. What malt is it?' he said.

'It's an ageing malt,' Harvey said.

They made their way up the stairs and into the office. Opening the doors of a cabinet, he chose to remove heavily cut glasses that he filled with ice. He then took a bottle of whisky and poured it into the glass. They chose to sit on low seating with a large low-level table before them.

'That tastes good,' said Varman taking a large slug of the drink.

'We are helping with the decorating of Janine's property this weekend,' said Harvey.

'Why can't we just get painters in?' he replied.

'She doesn't trust the painters with her doll collection.' Harvey replaced the empty, heavy glass on the table, and sat back to relax.

'She has had the doll for years,' said Varman.

'They are collectors' items,' said Harvey.

'So what is the plan, what time are we due to start there?' said Varman. A tall heavily built man with a full brawny torso, his lean face had bright blue eyes.

'We will start early in the morning so get an early night,' he said meaningfully.

'Who will get the paint?' Varman replied.

'You will have to get the paint yourself,' said Harvey.

'How will I know what colours to get?' he said.

'You will have to go and get Janine from the house and take her with you when you purchase the paint,' said Harvey.

'When shall I do that,' said Varman.

'We could do that this afternoon so that we are all ready for tomorrow morning.' Harvey collected the bottle of whisky. 'She also wants the bedrooms doing and the hallway and stairs.'

'She will have to move all of the furniture out of the way,' said Varman.

'We will just cover the furniture with blankets and be careful not to spill the paint everywhere.' Harvey poured himself a new glass of drink. 'We are also to check the sewing machine for the clothes, whilst I think,' said Harvey.

'We have been stitching on the fake logos at a steady rate,' said Varman.

'The sewing machine has malfunctioned, it just doesn't look as neat as it did,' said Harvey concerned. He looked at his watch, his hand had gold rings on.

'You are able to tell that they are fakes,' said Varman.

'You couldn't tell that they were fakes before,' said Harvey.

'You couldn't tell but you can now.' He leant forwards for the bottle. 'The packaging will cover it all.'

'You know what happens, they take it from the packaging and inspect it. The packaging will not resolve the problem,' said Harvey.

'I thought the packaging looked good, it has all of the holograms on and the labels are there,' said Varman.

'There is nothing wrong with the packaging, it's the sewing machines. The work has become shoddy and we have to fix it,' said Harvey. He returned his finished glass to the table.

'Perhaps it is the people using the machine,' said Varman. He looked at him through blue eyes, his short blond hair on his brow.

'It's the precision of the machine, it needs resetting,' said Harvey.

'We will have somebody in to service the machines,' replied Varman.

'The machines should be brand new after the service and the results will return.' He lifted his arm resting it on the back of the chair. 'When are we going to remove the boxes that are complete?'

'The shirts are all folded and in boxes already.' Varman said.

'They are all folded and in boxes ready to go, they require collecting,' said Harvey.

'I will go down there with a van and have them loaded and transported,' said Varman.

'That will free up space for the tracksuit tops,' he replied

'We have got a lot of tracksuit tops to shift.' Varman said.

'I know a person that will buy the lot from us so we won't get stuck with them for very long.' Harvey stood up from the chair, brushing his hands over his ill-fitting suit.

'Just let me know and we will deliver them for you Harvey.'

Chapter 12
Issy

Issy was a girl with natural mousey brown hair, she had a small face with a snout nose and lush plump cheeks. She raised her arm to receive an article of clothing from behind her. She thought of her new friend sitting comfortably in a soft chair waiting for her to change. She collected a long dress, and holding it draped before her, she touched the embroidery with her hands. She glimpsed through the edge of the finely carved ornate dress screen to the distant room to a bed with a figure. She lowered the soft article to the floor, and stepping into it, she pulled at the evening dress. Kirsten was taking care of her today while Denem slept. Issy stood barefoot to the cold dark walnut floor. Stepping out from the screen, she stood before the mirror viewing herself.

'Your body appears longer, and more slender, in that one,' Kirsten said. She sat with a cotton dress on her body.

'The dress makes me appear younger.' She raised her hands to touch to the dress.

'I think that you appear younger with more of your body on show.' Issy looked at the girl's choice of dress. She sat in a walnut chair with a cushion.

'What a tight dress.'

'What else do you think that I need.'

'You are able to look younger in many ways. You could use jewellery and make-up,' Kirsten said. Issy looked at the girls black hair held with a bright red bow.

'You are wrong, Kirsten, it is to display wealth, you appear older with jewellery,' she said. The brown dress on her slender body, she touched her neck for a necklace.

'If you are born wealthy then you can wear jewellery at any age,' Issy spoke dismissively.

'You are right.' She viewed her dress.

'Why do I care about wealth and why would I want to appear younger? I am very content with my knowledge for my age,' she said. Issy ran her hands along the sides of her dress.

Kirsten touched her mouth, and sighing, looked at a side table to grasp her crocodile skin wallet. She released the bag with a touch of a small silver clip opening to view the contents inside. She glanced at the dark blue bedroom with painted mural wallpaper. She collected her compact to view her large eyes before glancing to Issy. Issy disappeared behind the large ornate dress screen.

'I think that the other dress is better, Issy, I really do.' She looked at her under the light of the chandelier. She stood in a large room set with soft chairs above a heavy weave carpet, they viewed the bed.

'I like this dress, I don't want you think there is something wrong with it. Denem will like it, won't he?' she shouted over the screen.

'What do you like about him, Issy?' Kirsten sighed.

'He is asleep over there, he will hear us.' She peered out from the screen and viewed him lying on the bed. She wanted to be alone with him, and to understand him, she did not want to be with Kirsten and him together. She took a step from the screen wearing the new dress.

'I enjoy his manner with me and with others,' Kirsten said. She began to touch Issy's hair as she viewed the mirror.

'It is good that you consider how he is with others,' she

replied.

'I also enjoy watching him with others.' Kirsten leaned to take a glimpse of the mirror herself.

'I understand who I am with, I am always important but he corrects me in my thinking,' she said. Kirsten released her brown wispy hair from her hands.

'How is Denem to work with?'

'He is fine I enjoy being his aide,' said Kirsten.

'Have you worked with him for long?' she replied.

'I worked some place else, before.' She remembered her past. The blustering wind carried the rain against the side of the building, streaming water diagonally across the glass. SDhe sat close to the windows, allowing her to view between towers to the marina holding small vessels with masts. The boats swayed in the blizzard and the waves collected over them, washing water to their decks. She viewed the figures on the screens before signing the slips of paper and returning her gaze to the monitors. She returned her gaze to Issy.

'Where was it that you worked?' Issy said.

'It was an investors' that I worked at, before Denem found me and gave me this job at his investor's.'

'Lucky you, Denem is great,' Issy said.

'Yes, he quite good to work for,' Kirsten replied.

They looked at Denem sleeping on the large king bed with carved twisting posts and an ornate canopy.

'There, I am going to the bed to visit him.' She moved across the room, slowing as she got to him. Kirsten followed her.

'He is sleeping, we should join him later when he wakes,' Kirsten whispered. Her wild dark eyes took him in longingly, and Issy touched his heavy, soft brown hair lightly, with her hand.

'I want to sit with him now.'

They approached the bed slowly and slipped themselves on top of the covers. He turned and opened his large green eyes. He reached out and touched Issy.

'What made you choose this colour dress?'

'The embroidery, it is carefully stitched.' Issy touched it with her fingertips. 'The gold stars are delicately detailed and their trails twist and entwine to a beautiful pattern.'

'They are not stars they are gold vines with leaves if you look carefully,' Kirsten said.

'I like your hair too, you have done it in a different way,' he said.

'I don't really like my hair, it is not heavy enough. I want it thicker and heavier.' She touched a wispy strand on her forehead.

'Where are you going Kirsten, come over here and sit with us on the bed,' he hollered across the blue room to her as she began to move away.

'I was just going, I am to meet someone,' she said. She hesitated at the door beside blue finely painted wallpaper.

'He wants me to be with him here' she said. 'You have Issy.'

'You are shouting across the room to me, join me on the bed,' he demanded.

Chapter 13
Aston

He dressed in a black suit with sharp trousers. His jacket was over a white shirt. Small pearlescent buttons revealed from the sleeve of the suit jacket. He wore a bow tie.

'You will enjoy those attending, we are to use the whole property, every room,' Denem said.

'I am so excited to be going with you,' she replied.

'I will remain with you as much as possible, Issy, you will be beside me.' He viewed a red fabric flower clipped to her hair.

'Stay with us, do not be with anyone else.' She tilted her head.

'There are a great many people to speak with so it may be difficult.' He looked at Issy's dark eyes. 'There are many rooms.' He pulled at her arm with a chuckle.

'We will visit the rooms together,' she said.

'Pass through the rooms with me and enjoy each of them.' He touched her snub nose gently. 'You are able to view the terrace from a number of the rooms and join me there if you want.'

'What do you remember most about a person?' she said. Wild wispy hair covered her forehead.

'I remember how they are when we met.' He viewed her through green eyes. 'You remember their appearance.'

'I remember their manner,' she replied.

'How do you want them to be?' he said, staring at her.

'I want them to be proud and confident.' She stood upright with her hands by her side.

'How about alluring and thoughtful?'

'That sounds good, a little like you.' She poked a friendly finger at him.

'Show us your gown,' he said.

'Do you like the silk gown that I chose for you? It is covered with fine embroidery,' she replied, holding it out before her.

'I like the gown. It is good to see you in it and all dressed up ready,' he replied.

'What makes a great person, Denem, before we go?' she said.

'They are great when you appreciate them,' he replied.

'They also have to appreciate you.' She tilted to her head and smirked.

'That would be finding someone that cares.' He smiled back to her.

'I may have done just that,' she said.

'My family are present for most of the evening you should speak to them.' He raised a hand to his belt. 'Many of them will be there.'

'I will be able to meet with them all,' she replied happily.

He beamed at her through straight white teeth. Issy clutched to his arm as he passed through an oak door. An ornate spiralling stair with bronze handrail took them downstairs.

'Listen, before we go in here, you are to remain away from Gerald. He sells cars and I do not want you with him until he has spoken to Aston,' Denem demanded.

'We might want to speak with him, Denem, if he has cars,' Issy replied.

'Speak with others, there are many different people here. You may be able to meet him later,' he said.

'It seems a funny reason, I usually speak with who I want,'

she said defiantly, thinking that she wanted a car.

'There are others that are fun, I am undertaking business with him, just do as I ask,' he said, getting annoyed but knowing that he had bought her a present. He turned to the stairs and Issy linked her slender arm beneath his. They navigated the stairs her hand passing across the handrail.

Large oak doors to the carpeted lobby opened to high windows and a smooth stark white ceiling. A large fireplace with a stone surround stood centred to a wall. Soft chairs were arranged above a heavy weave carpet and the walls had portraits. The room filled with people, standing with glasses in their hands. A filled terrace above a long, landscaped garden stood beyond.

'Shall we visit those pair just there.' He tugged at Issy's arm.

'We could pass over them,' she replied.

He passed a pair holding drinks. He viewed a tall girl with a thin, gaunt face, her hair short and blonde. She wore large white rimmed sunglasses. A man beside her with a similar appearance gave a meaningful smirk at Denem.

'Hello, how are you?' he said.

'We are both fine,' Denem replied, his green captivating eyes upon them. His large, sturdy, pale hands at his side, a thin gold watch at his wrist.

'They are a fine pair of sunglasses on your face,' said Issy.

'I always wear sunglasses at this time of the year, the sun is low and bright,' said the woman, lifting her hand to her head.

'They go well with what you are wearing,' Issy said.

'This suit was especially prepared for the sunglasses.' She laughed.

'I am sure it was,' Denem said. 'How are you?'

'I am fine, the event is a success,' said the man standing with them. People surrounded them.

'There are a great deal more people here than I expected I must speak with them all,' Denem replied.

'Good luck with that,' said the women. 'We will remain here.'

'I would stay and speak but I am to move to that group there.' He pointed to Aston standing on the terrace. Aston stood with the breeze moving his hair. Admiring the property, he considered some of his own. A large cottage stood at the end of a long field beside a river with a waterwheel. It was on the outskirts of the town and was always quiet. He would look at the property and consider what it might be like to live there with his family. He walked across to the window of the cottage to look inside. He noticed that one of the small window panes that formed a larger picture window had been broken. Peering through, he looked into a dark room filled with cobwebs and decaying carpet that was pulled back to reveal a magnificent stone floor. He returned his gaze to Denem. He stood in a group beside Aston by the terrace wall. Denem took his green eyes meaningfully upon him with a small sincere smirk viewing the hard features of Aston's face. He was dressed in a fine dark-green suit, with a white shirt, and his toned arms opened in front of him, to greet to his friend.

'You are looking good, Denem,' he said.

'Is Dora with you this evening,' Denem replied.

'I'm at the event alone, Dora couldn't make it,' he said.

'Why couldn't she make it, I would have liked to have seen her,' Issy replied.

'She had to stay at home,' he said.

'How is the house?'

'We are repairing the country house and she wants to renovate a number of the rooms with decorators and it had to happen today to stop delays to the schedule.' He widened his eyes, and with a caring look at Denem, raised his arm to his shoulder.

'I want to see Dora, it has been a while,' he said.

'She wants you to have dinner with us,' said Aston.

'Tell her that dinner is a good idea,' he replied.

'Come to the new house next month, and take a look at it.' He remembered the property again. The back door was accessed through bushes of stinging nettles that he waded through carefully. He grew up in a large city and he enjoyed the idea of owning a country property in addition to the many townhouses that he had already built up as part of his portfolio. Many of the houses he filtered money through in the form of lease holding payments that he received from the occupants. Upon reaching the back door, he noticed that the bottom panel had been removed. There were two men inside the property. Returning to his car he collected a shotgun. He loaded the cylinder with cartridges and made his way into the house. Denem passed a warm smirk at him, lifting his sturdy hand to rest to Aston's back. Issy standing beside him took Aston's attention. She was short with a small snub nose and wispy, brown hair.

'Who is that, Denem?' Aston said with a thickly muffled tone.

'We began to speak when I was shopping,' he smirked. 'Her name is Issy,' he said.

'She seems a nice girl, she is speaking with everybody,' he said.

'We were shopping together, she is a newspaper reporter,' Denem replied.

'What has she reported on?' Aston said.

'She reported on the recent jewellery store heist with the burly city boys,' Denem said through straight white teeth. He touched to his black silk jacket. 'We have spent the past few afternoons together to the bedroom area.'

'She is quite tasteful,' Aston replied.

'She is passionate about her work. She doesn't stop speaking about it,' Denem said.

'I will have to speak with her and find out more about her,' said Aston.

'It is off-putting, a person does not always want to speak about another person's work,' said Denem.

'What will you plan for her?' he said.

'I will see her for a few more months and understand her more to see if I like her.' Denem said viewing them through green eyes. He raised a large sturdy hand turning to Aston, resting it on the back of his soft cotton dark green suit jacket. His eyes passed to the fireplace beyond.

'So you are friends with Denem.'

'I am his aide.'

'What did you do when you were last together.'

'We walked through the garden where we live and it is beside a forest, there is a garden house that we sit. We shouldn't out of season, but we sit there together and have done for many years. We even watch the snow fall there, he is a close friend of my wife, Dora.'

She looked at the worn complexion of his face and his broad flat nose.

'You understand each other then. What do you like most about Denem and then I will tell you what I like most about him myself,' she said.

'He is good with answers. He knows what I need to know,' Aston replied.

'I think he is good with questions, you discover yourself with him.' She fluttered her eyelashes and chuckled, lowering her chin a little. 'That is because you work for him right, you have to get information from him and make decisions.' She looked t up to him, composing herself.

'He is fun, he is good to speak with. We speak about everything. I have known him for a long time.' He stared at her with blue eyes and flat cheeks.

'He makes me think about my answers and I usually discover something small about myself.' Her tone was intimate.

'He is a great man.'

Chapter 14
Gerald

Cathy and Kirsten passed to the terrace from the hall through the finely carved timber doors.

They passed alongside a garden wall to stand beside Denem. The long garden held finely manicured flower beds, and a pathway through its centre that led to a large lake. He came close to Cathy's opal face focusing on her thin lips and she passed her hand to rest open upon his soft tailored suit jacket.

'Cathy you are looking good,' he said.

'Thank you, Denem,' she replied.

'The city that we just moved to is going to build a new nightlife, Denem,' said Cathy. She turned to Denem with large blue eyes.

'There are new groups of people that are moving because of new housing and they are wealthy,' said Kirsten.

'We know we are building some of the buildings.' They were working on the buildings at his investor's.

'There are smart new cafes and clubs,' Denem said.

'If she wants to go and meet others then they are likely to be at that location beside the coast to a number of clubs,' said Kirsten.

'You should come with us, Denem, one night, she doesn't always go but I go with my friends and I enjoy it,' said Cathy touching the sleeve of his jacket.

'I will consider it,' he said.

'That is a nice jacket that you are wearing.' Kirsten said,

viewing him, and admiring his angular face and his heavy hair.

'You would look good in it,' he replied.

'Do you think?' She imagined herself wearing it. 'Without anything else at all on me, is that what you think.' She laughed rudely.

'I saw you in the window earlier,' he said. 'I was watching you.'

'I sat here earlier, were you able to see me from the windows up there amongst all of these people?' She turned her body and pointed to a row of windows behind her. 'Why were you up there, you should have been down here with your guests.'

'Those rooms are also open, there are others enjoying them now. They are eating in the rooms on the upper level.' Denem beamed through straight white teeth.

'What are they eating up there for?' Kirsten said.

'The rooms are better and the food gets cold down here, they are able to sit at a number of large tables,' he said.

'Let's go to those rooms.' Cathy said again. 'I am able to see them eating at the windows.'

'I am here with Issy, I cannot go to the rooms right now Cathy,' he said. 'I also have to worry about my guests.'

From the door, Denem looked for the rounded face of Gerald. He had a short dark beard shaped and pointed to his chin. He stood wearing a deep green cotton suit and passed Denem a sly smirk. Denem beamed straight white teeth in return.

'Gerald, these are my friends, speak with them, you might know them,' Denem said.

'He specialises in cars, we were together at her friend's property, you had a gold car,' said Cathy.

'You are the guy from before,' said Kirsten. 'I remember you.'

'I remember we also viewed the cars together before,' said Gerald. He opened his arms wide to them.

'Have you got one with you today? Show it to us if you have,' Kirsten cried out eagerly.

'What do you want to look at, do you have a favourite to view to?' He focused upon the girls before him. A large fireplace beside them had writhing flames and glowing red embers.

'When we met before you were telling us about your boat trip and how you became stranded on an island whilst you were collecting your cars.'

'Cars ship from the mainland everybody knows this,' Denem said with a frown. 'He wasn't on an island purchasing cars, he is telling stories as usual.' He touched his belt. A smartly dressed couple passed between them. 'We have to speak at some point about this, Gerald.'

'I am getting it for you, Denem.' He shrugged his broad shoulders. 'You will be happy when you receive the car, the photographs just do not do it justice.'

'Issy is here I do not want you mentioning it to her if she speaks with you,' he growled. 'It is a gift for her at some point.'

'Talk about where you go Gerald to get your cars,' Cathy pleaded. Gerald leaned forward taking his arm around her to get her attention.

'The cars are shipped across the Atlantic, they are registered here and distributed,' Gerald's said, with blue meaningful eyes.

'We want to see a car, the best that you have,' Kirsten said.

'I have a car with me today,' Gerald replied. 'You will hold the keys in my pocket later on this evening if you are lucky.' He removed his empty hand teasing her.

'Where is it?' Cathy said. 'I viewed your cars already when we met before, show me the car now, allow me a glimpse,' she said. Holding the attention of them both, he sighed and slowly returned his hand to his pocket grasping the keys. Removing them, he uncurled his large fingers.

'I want those keys from you, Gerald, that is what you have on order for me the car that you are holding the keys for,' Denem cried. He turned to view him dressed in a fine black evening suit.

'There they are,' Gerald cried dangling the keys.

'That is my car, Denem, yours is to order,' Gerald said.

'You owed me the money for a long time, and I want the car as a present for a special person, a girl that I know.' Denem took the keys with a quick swipe through the air. 'This car will do me just fine.' Gerald took an urgent step forwards and Aston grasped his arm. He turned with a furrowed brow, viewing the poe-faced man staring at him.

'Allow him the car, Gerald, you owe him it,' Aston mumbled in his ear.

'Here, take a look, Denem, yours is similar to that and it is on order,' said Gerald. Aston grasped his arm. 'Actually, just keep it,' he said, changing his mind.

'There should not be delays like there were,' Denem howled with the set of keys clenched in his hand. He threw the keys to Issy. She gazed to the them with her eyes wide.

'Here, a present,' he said.

'Really?' replied Issy, surprised.

'I am getting him a car, why, does he also wants to take that one?' Gerald said. He stepped away from the group and his foot caught on the leg of a large mahogany chair, and he fell forwards. Aston raised his hand to steady him. Gerald flew towards the fire, past the large white decorative surround where he lay to upon the ground. He struggled and his arm and shoulders caught some embers. From his side he kneeled before them struggling to his feet, with Aston helping. He stood with black marks on his open hands and clothing.

'You fell Gerald, take him to the hall to ready himself,' Denem howled directing him away with his hand. A waiter guided him to the lobby.

'What is happening, this is to stop,' Kirsten said.

'Take him out of here,' said Denem.

'Kirsten, there is little reason for you to worry, we have this resolved.' Aston signalled with a large worn hand to the smartly dressed man being led away. Denem turned his angular head to inspect the fire and he signalled to a waiter to clear the glowing embers. Kirsten stepped forwards from behind a man in evening wear who was standing, watching.

'We do not see each other enough, you should visit the office and sit down with us there, occasionally,' Aston said to Kirsten.

'She is my aide and I keep her busy, she is with me most of the day and it will be difficult for her to find the time,' Denem replied. He took a large open hand across the lapel of his jacket.

'We are busy visiting various locations to monitor our investments,' Kirsten said. 'I was meant to visit the other day and the meeting was cancelled.'

'We are taking new projects everywhere. She travels with me and we enjoy our days together,' Denem said. He turned to a couple standing beside him. They stood dressed in fine evening gowns and suits.

'Your garden is filled with wild flowers, they are an amazing azure blue,' said the women focusing beyond the French doors.

'They grow in only a number of locations in the country, mainly in escarpments and we decided to plant them before the rocks in the garden,' Denem said. 'I dislike flowers in the home but I knew that many would enjoy them this evening so I arranged for some to be picked.' He pointed to an arrangement of the flowers on a table.

'Why do you not like flowers when they appear as beautiful as that?' said the women. Her husband linked her arm.

'Flowers should remain outside in the garden but on this occasion, I requested they pick them for us all,' Denem said.

'They appear beautiful, they should be enjoyed,' the man replied.

'I like to pass them on a country walk,' Denem said.

'We should all picnic beside them in the summer with a wicker basket and a blanket,' the women suggested.

'We will sit together and view them swaying in the breeze. They are all over the ground down there.' Denem agreed. The couple passed to another beside them and they began to speak.

Chapter 15
Denem

Denem wore to a fine dark grey textured suit tight to his body with four black swirling ivory buttons on the jacket sleeve. He sat at a table in a bar close to the city centre.

'I suggest we sit here at this table, we could make the decision of going further into the quieter areas if we wanted to,' he said.

'Do you know that girl with him, I recognise them.' Issy pointed with her finger to a girl passing beside them.

'She visits the club. The girl was spoken to when we visited here last,' he said.

'We should go over there and speak with her,' she declared.

'We are quite happy sitting here.'

Issy stood up from the low seater, and with a look over her shoulder to Denem, she took her hand to flick her wispy brown hair. She wore a tight dress and strode on high heels.

'Who are you?' the girl said when she approached her.

'We have a table over there. You could sit with us, I recognise you from before,' Issy said.

'I am content remaining with my group,' said the girl. Issy returned to the table.

'I was quite happy sitting here with you.' Denem took hold to a heavy cut tumbler and he took a sip.

'I am happy sitting here with you, also.' She touched her wispy brown hair. 'I just thought that I recognised her.'

'They prepared the table with flowers, they are amazing. The scent fills the room.' He raised a pale hand over the flowers.

'They are nice,' she said, standing to lean over them and inspect them.

'View the mixture of rich colours and textures in the glass vase,' Denem said.

'They are colourful.' She touched a petal with her fingertips. 'We want Champagne, Denem, order me Champagne, please,' she said.

'Get her some Champagne,' he said to the waiter. The tall waiter in casual clothing scribbled a note on a pad and moved away from the table.

'The afternoons at the house, do you enjoy them?' Denem said. He leant his arm across the back of the chair.

'There are afternoons when we are together that I would rather be with no one else.' She touched the soft weave of his sleeve. He thought of Stephanie as she touched him.

'This group will approach the table.' He raised a finger to point. 'They wish to speak with me.'

'Shall we go to a private room if you do not want to speak with them? I do not really like them, they are often at the club often.' She raised her slender hand to wave them away.

'You know Kylie, the girl with blonde hair,' he said.

'She has it tied into pigtails this evening, I think I recognise her,' said Issy.

'She sat with me here before,' he said.

The drinks arrived at the table and the waiter placed the sparkling straw-coloured drinks on paper coasters.

'Shall we enjoy a drink together.' He lifted a hand to the table.

'I am not sure that I want that, Denem,' she replied.

'I have just ordered it.' He gazed over his shoulder for a

waiter.

'I want something different,' she said.

'You asked for Champagne,' he said, becoming annoyed.

'I have changed my mind I don't want it.' He remembered ordering drinks with Stephanie, she was never such a problem.

'I will change it for you.' He raised a hand and the waiter took the drink away.

'You should change it.' She crossed her arms.

'What do you want instead?' he asked.

'I will drink a martini with a cherry.' She raised her hand above the table.

'Bring me one of those, please.' The waiter hurried away.

'I don't remember things being so difficult, Issy,' he said. She didn't reply instead she lifted her skin wallet and fumbled for her telephone. Eventually she spoke.

'I've got to do that thing with work.'

'We are enjoying our evening, what do you have to do with work?' he said.

'I have to go in early tomorrow morning, and take photographs so I cannot be late tonight.' She touched her brown wispy hair.

'That is not very well organised of you,' he replied, becoming annoyed.

'What do you mean?' she said.

'You knew that we were spending the evening together and that we were going to the club.' He passed his large green eyes over her.

'There is nothing I can do about it, I have to work,' she said.

'There is something that you could have done. You could have organised it for a different day,' he said wishing that he was with Stephanie. They never had discussions like this.

'I'm not sure that I like all of these people around us.'

'We could remain here and speak more if you like, or we could consider going to a different room,' Denem cried. 'There are private rooms with improved views across the city.'

'We will go to those rooms,' she said

'We could go to the rooms but it is not necessary, there is hardly anyone here.'

'There's a few here that will bother us,' she said.

'Do you know them.' Denem raised a large hand to point.

'I don't really know them,' she said.

'I know of these people through others,' Denem said. He stared at them.

'How are you, David?' He raised a hand to him. He approached the table. He wore a loose shirt beneath a jacket and his tight trousers clung to his legs. He had a scarf that wrapped around his neck. 'We were in contact before, you were at a party at a large house on the outskirts of the city,' Denem said.

'Yes, I was at a party,' the man replied.

'We had the terrace open and there were fireworks,' he said lifting a pale hand.

'We had a great evening, I really enjoyed the ice sculptures,' said the man.

'They were quite something, I am glad that you enjoyed them,' said Denem.

'We will have to meet again,' he said touching the scarf loosely wrapped to his neck.

'We are throwing another party in a couple of weeks' time,' Issy said.

'We will attend, for sure. I am going over there to speak to somebody else.' He strode away from the table towards a group of men drinking at the bar.

Tall grey angular chairs were in a line in front of the bar counter and shiny metal sheeting was across the ceiling and walls. Denem, seated, looked into the distance through a tall window across a roof garden with lush green plants and tall leafy trees.

'I recieved a gift from a man,' said Issy.

'Who was it from?' Denem said.

'I cannot say.' She covered her mouth with her hand.

'Well don't then,' he said.

'I received a gift of scent from a male friend that I visited many years ago. I forgot all about him and he delivered the parcel to my residence.' Issy looked at him meaningfully.

'That was nice of him.' He thought of Stephanie and wished she was with him instead.

'I am going to begin wearing it,' she said.

'You can wear it if you want.'

'It may remind me of him though,' she replied.

'It will remind you of him,' he said.

'He is from the city, I wonder why he remembered me enough to send a gift like that?' She touched her hair and it fell across her forehead.

'It is a brash and impolite scent, is that what you want?' Denem said.

'What does that mean?' She chuckled. 'It is brash, and impolite, it is very strong smelling.'

'What does it remind you of?' he said

'It reminds me of the past,' she replied.

'I expect that he passed to you a light floral scent without thought.' He reached forward for his drink.

'What do you mean by that,' she said,

'It is all in the past, they will fade away.'

'Well, he is not fading for me. I have got scent.' She touched her neck with her fingertips.

A group of men approached the table wearing to smart suits.

'Who are you sitting here with, we know her,' said the man.

'It's Issy, you met her before,' Denem replied.

'We speak all the time here, don't we Issy?' said the man touching to his lapel.

'We speak occasionally, when I am here at the club,' she said.

'Did you want to come with us to the private rooms?' his friend said, looking to the door.

'I am not interested this evening, I am with him.' She touched Denem's arm.

'Leave it. We are together,' said Denem.

'I could go with them if I wanted,' she said.

'You could go with them, but we would not be friends any more, Issy.' Denem passed green eyes over her with a furrowed brow.

'I will go with them a different time.'

'Maybe a different time is better.' He didn't remember any of these problems with Stephanie.

'We are there if you want us. Just come and find us.' The two men began to walk from the table.

'Bye for now,' Denem said.

'They were nice don't you think, Denem,' she said.

'They are known to me, I do not often bother speaking with them,' he replied.

'Forget about them. What makes a moment to remember?' She touched his shoulder.

'When it is shared with a person that cares.' Denem removed her hair from her cheek.

'What do I have to do to make you care.' She pointed to him.

'I care for everyone, but when we are with a person that cares,, it becomes love,' he said.

'So we are finding love,' she replied.

'We are trying to find love,' he replied.

'No way, look who is coming now,' she said covering her face with her hand.

'What is wrong?'

'This group began to touch me roughly once before at the club, they wanted to take me from here.' She huddled into him.

'We could speak with them but there are too many of them. We need Aston here,' said Denem

'The girl that is also with them, is awful,' she said.

'She looks good with that long plait of blonde hair resting on her torso, and that tight shiny catsuit.'

'He is taking an interest in your figure,' the man said as he passed the table.

'I am taking an interest in her catsuit,' Denem said.

'She is mine. I take interest in her figure,' the man replied.

'I'll not enjoy the company of these men, I told you that he was scary when I visited before,' Issy said, cuddling up to Denem.

'We remember you from before,' the man said.

'They surrounded me in the club before,' she replied. Denem sat forwards.

'We saw her in here the other week, it is all fine now,' said the man.

'Where did you go to, didn't you like them touching you?' Her glossy catsuit was taut on her figure.

'These guys can be a pain,' said the girl.

'You were grabbing at me and I do not enjoy to your

company, what do you want with me?' said Issy.

'She is with me. We are sitting here,' Denem said.

'Come on, we will find someone else to speak to.' The group moved away from the table.

'Who were they, stay away from people like that Issy,' he said.

'I will, I have got you to protect me,' she replied touching his leg.

Chapter 16
Suliam

The painted fabric of the screens on the walls of the lobby shone with a warm light and a side window gave views over gravel courtyards filled with lush verdure and branches carrying berries and ripe fruit. Denem viewed through the large glass doors of the restaurant to a tall fair-faced man with a head of brilliant white hair, his large round eyes were piercing blue and his nose was prominent. He wore a uniform of a stiff blue suit, with a white shirt beneath, a firm handkerchief folded in his pocket. As they waited, Denem, raising his hand, got the attention of a nearby waiter.

'The walls of the lobby are a hand-painted fabric that I enjoy but they require changing, the panels are beginning to fade.' Denem said. 'They are a mess and you have guests that pass through that lobby and I eat here regularly. I always have to mention the decor to you.' He viewed the large expansive white room beyond with a low ceiling and hanging lamps. He watched Jonnie Suliam as he moved slowly from the window to his chair beside a large rectangular beech table.

'I'll organise the changes to be made and someone will undertake the work,' said the tall thin waiter clutching a flat silver tray in his hand.

'Just get the décor right, you walk through here each day it should not require me to tell you. I am always here with a large group of people and it has to right for me.' Denem walked towards the large table with the waiter following behind him, listening. 'I just won't come here any more,' he cried to him over his shoulder. He strode on long legs with his brown hair to the side, a tailored suit with a white shirt revealing his chest. A jacket sleeve held with ivory buttons, revealed a thin gold watch, glimpsed from his sleeve.

'Are you ready to meet with them, Denem?' said Kirsten

'Come on then, Kirsten, join me now.' Denem viewed her waiting patiently for him beside the brasserie doors gazing upon paintings on the walls. She began to walk beside him, her fitted wool dress, tight on her body, a gold broach with jewels glistened on her front. She had been his assistant for two years and she was becoming increasingly tolerant of the man and his reactions. She clutched a portfolio that held the investments that they were to discuss today with the waiting table.

'It's good to see you all.' He spoke with his arms raised and his hands open with flared fingers. He approached the table where a large blonde girl was sitting, wearing blue baggy denim dungarees, her face with soft rounded features and blue eyes. She peered through the window of a finely decorated cake box held with ink motifs of ivy leaves and berries.

'It's great to meet with you all,' said Kirsten, her straight black hair across her oval face rested on her neck. 'We have got lots to discuss.'

Jonnie Suliam was an ageing financier that knew the industry, he had been involved in deals in the city for most of his life. She had planned to meet with him on a few occasions throughout the previous year but he had always cancelled or sent a somebody different. This was the first time that she had arranged for the men to be together. Denem's large hand unbuttoned his suit jacket, and with a pinch of his sharp trousers, he sat.

'The surroundings that you chose to meet are good,' Suliam growled a tone from his throat.

'We have all of the details of the investments with us,' said Emily. Her face had a pale yellow floral silk band thoughtfully folded and tied in a knot across her forehead. 'We are interested in the towers to the sea islands that you are able to see from here.' She pointed to the window with a rounded hand.

'Did you see them before from this location? They are quite a sight.' Denem viewed Emily through green eyes as she stood in blue cotton dungarees, and black, soft, leather lace-up boots to explain the scheme that Suliam wanted to invest into.

'The large tower that you view over there, you are able to visit and go up to the top levels where there is a brasserie allowing views along the coast,' said Kirsten.

'The brasserie is good here, they take real care of the food, there is another on the corner, that I also love,' Emily replied. She viewed the distant towers from the window, considering her favourite place, and then to around the room at the white décor. 'This one I think is better.'

'The silk band on your head is something special.' Denem beamed at her through straight white teeth from his angular face and she smirked in return, admiring to his dark brown hair.

'This, do you think,' she said as she lifted a heavy hand to touch to the floral silk band held across her short spiky bleached-blonde hair.

'The band pulls your hair back and helps in accentuating the features of your face,' he said. His mesmerising green eyes rested to upon her bulbous figure through the loose baggy cotton of her dungarees.

'It may be the choice of material that the band is made from, it is the colour and the shiny nature of the silk against the tone of my skin.' Her rounded fingertips passed across the silk band to her head. Her eyes suddenly widened with surprise as she remembered the occasion. 'It is my birthday today,' she explained with her hands raised before her, excitedly. 'Everybody, it is my birthday.' She then clapped her hands together excitedly before herself.

'It is your birthday today and you are choosing to enjoy it with us,' Kirsten said, as she reached forwards to pull the finely decorated cake box closer to her to view the contents. She peered into the cake box standing on the table, and the cake inside covered in delicious glistening sugar fondant. 'It is a bright pink cake and it appears finely decorated I cannot wait to eat it with you.'

Hearing a squeal and raising her head, she watched as a waiter passed through the large glass doors to the brasserie with them stopping hard against the wall. 'What is happening there?' Kirsten viewed Denem, and followed him as he turned to his head.

'There is a fire,' shrieked a waitress clutching a large silver tray in her hand. 'There is a fire on the screens in the hall, collect water.'

The doors closed behind her and in the distance yellow flames could be viewed with the outline of a man releasing foam from an extinguisher. Smoke bellowed everywhere.

'I hope they sort that out or we will all have to leave,' said Kirsten, concerned.

'It is only a small fire they will handle it,' Denem bellowed, knowing that Aston had visited to satisfy himself about the screens in the entrance lobby.

'Strange how these things happen isn't it Denem,' said Suliam. He gazed toward the smoky room at the far end of the restaurant and began to remember his past. He sat calmly before the screens as the explosions in the city started. People began to run from the buildings. Men running to the buildings to help became hurt, with the second explosion blowing them out of view of the camera that he was looking at. The street lay still and dust collecting in the air began to settle. He removed a small black earpiece from his ear and stood up from his chair.

'You will all enjoy that birthday cake and you will gain weight,' Jonnie Suliam said pointing to the cake. 'Emily enjoys her cake, she is always ordering cake,' he spoke, to take his mind away from his past thoughts.

'Are you saying that there is weight on me, Jonnie Suliam? I care about your thoughts very much but my body is my body and I enjoy cake very much.' She giggled. 'There is nothing wrong with that body, I have a desirable figure that I love.' Emily, standing, watched as a waiter opened the cake box and lifted the large cake onto the table before removing the blue and silver wrapping on its outside.

'The cake looks good, I do not want any, though,' Kirsten said seductively. She collected her hand on her own torso that held firm and tight.

'My belly is wanting some of this, for sure.' A lively tone passed from Emily. 'That appears luscious and there is plenty for everyone.' She stood and cutting slices of the cake, she touched her rounded hand above her soft baggy blue cotton dungarees that covered her weighty hips.

'How are you feeling about your birthday?' said Jonnie Suliam, raising a greying brow.

'I feel no emotion whatsoever about it. I always meet with my group of friends to celebrate. I honestly didn't really think about it too much,' Emily said.

'Emotions are interesting, they are always achieved from a thought defined by you, you control them,' Denem hollered. She viewed his large bewildering green eyes in his angular face and across his solemn hair.

'Or a person could be controlling your thoughts to make an emotion,' Suliam said in a low tone.

'Or they control them with a touch, they make contact with you.' Emily said passing a look across to Denem. 'I love contact with others.'

'What about when a person pinches you,' Denem said. 'A real hard pinch.'

'I don't get emotional over pinches,' she quickly stated, turning away from him. 'Pinches mean that you don't like me.'

'A pinch can be playful, if it's not too hard,' Denem replied. They returned to the cake.

'I hope you all enjoy it.' Emily pointed to her thin pink slice of cake held with iced piped dots on the edge of the round cake with a serviette folded beside. 'I am eating this cake because of the chocolatier, a friend recommended it on twenty-second and west off of the boulevard.' She ate a mouthful of cake from her fork and bounced it on the plate, rolling her eyes delectably. Across the busy brasserie, a man with a cowboy hat passed between seated diners. He strode confidently, wearing a heavy white leather jacket over a cotton shirt with an ornate belt buckle in the shape of an eagle. Kirsten turned her head.

'Who is that man that is crossing the room his appearance is distinct, I almost recognise him.'

His bright gleaming eyes passed to the group with a meaningful beam from white teeth as he approached close to the large beech table.

'I know you from before,' she spoke to him seductively.

'It is Jenson, he said that he would attend if could,' said Denem, relieved that he could make it. They would now be able to talk seriously about their investments. Jenson was a wealthy man and held many contacts through the country.

'I will tell you now, there is plenty to discuss with you Jon.' He stood before the table and rested a large hand on his belt buckle. He passed bright gleaming eyes at the group from his broad, tanned face. He lifted a leg over the bench and took a seat beside Jonnie Suliam. 'I will have you know that we hold the island costing, you have the costs, we should discuss that today, we cannot waste any more time.' He viewed the large table with plates of pink cake covered with fondant. They planned to build new islands and to then build towers upon them.

Kirsten, turning her body from the group, took a call and began to speak into the telephone handset. Stopping the call and returning it to rest upon the surface of the table, she turned to Denem, casting her blue opal eyes to rest seriously upon him.

'Aston is requesting that I meet with someone at the hotel, I do not know why he scheduled the meeting, he knew that we were here together, I am a little annoyed that he double booked.' She touched his arm with a hand of pink painted nails, her wrist had a silver chain.

'I will return to the hotel, do you have everything that you need?' Kirsten stood touching her black straight hair with her fingertips. 'I am to depart, unfortunately.' Denem leant forwards to her, steadying himself with a large, graceful hand.

'I want to speak with them privately about the script before I depart today,' he whispered.

Emily turned her head to view them with a furrowed brow.

'Calm down, Denem, it will be fine to speak with them more,' she said tilting her head close to him, with her blue eyes on the table. 'I am for a different meeting, Denem will remain with you and continue to enjoy the food.' Kirsten looked up to the window, with a view of the city towers beyond. 'I wish you all the best.' She gave a quick glance over her shoulder, passing reassuring blue eyes to Denem.

'I want to talk about the script now. It is definitely what we want.' He wanted to access a hidden bank vault, the script would allow him to access great sums of money. He turned his head to the table, his broad shoulders beneath his grey suit jacket. 'I want to know what is happening with the script, I was promised it as part of the deal,' said Denem. Jonnie Suliam viewed the angular features of the face.

'We are finished, Denem, with that, we will not change our minds, the script will not pass to you.' Jonnie Suliam passed him a meaningful look. Denem, with a deep breath banged a graceful hand on the table and pointed a finger at Jonnie Suliam.

'I want a further meeting with you in a side room, now, away from the group, I will not accept that the script is sold.' He frowned his eyes at the ageing man with gritted straight teeth.

'You have it, we decided that together, and we spoke about this already.' Jenson turned his head slowly at the bang, looking through bright blue gleaming eyes at Jonnie Suliam and then turned to glare at Denem. The waiter, passing with cups balanced on a silver tray to above his shoulder, dropped a cup on the floor and it smashed. They chose to ignore it.

'There was a suggestion that you would let me have it, I want to be able to use the key generated long code allowing me access to the vault.' Denem gave a slow expectant smirk. Jonnie Suliam stood from the table, putting a large hand on his suit jacket, closing it at the button. He strode to the large window and he opened it further with a push from his hand to view the distant towers. He considered his past again.

The man lay bleeding from his ears, the blast had rendered him deaf. His hands hung by the sides of his head. A large group of schoolchildren stood shocked and crying, their teacher collecting them all in a group together. Other people ran for cover, half bent over and covering their heads with their hands. He stood from his chair and lifted to his telephone to call from his table.

'We are finished here, Denem, with this conversation, the script is not coming to you through us, we were not able to access the vaults anyway but perhaps the gentlemen that it has been left with will be luckier.' Jenson's tanned broad face bared to clenched teeth and his eyes glared at him.

'Everybody relax, we are all on a sugar low, that is why we are argumentative, eat more cake,' she declared with a chuckle. The group at the table became quiet and continued eating their cake, slowly.

'You are able to view the coral along the coast from here, you are able to see it as the large grey area outlined beneath the water,' said Suliam from the window

'The coral steps outward in the area beside that tower, the sea appears vivid blue.' They all gazed towards the window.

'You have it, I am able to view the coral it is quite a sight.' Senator Jenson's calm tone carried to Jonnie Suliam beside the window, who turned to look at him, viewing his blond hair, heavy and full on his shoulders and across his broad face, tanned with a trimmed beard around his small mouth.

'I walked beside the corals and they are in shallow waters, you can also see that there is a change in depth from that point of the sea.' Emily ran her fat stubby finger out in front of her in a line to the distance.

'It is a healthy reef, it has lots of marine life,' Jonnie Suliam bellowed. They turned to view his distinguished face with blue eyes. 'The fish that surround the reef, are brightly coloured a friend choses to dive there occasionally.'

'I would consider diving there myself.' Emily's tone carried. She collected herself beside Denem, and smelling his scent from his clothes, she reached her hand thoughtfully inside her bag to collect an address card.

Chapter 17
Janine

The large white house was accessed through large black metal gates that led to a driveway with shrubs and tall leafy trees that surrounded the house. Harvey sat in an armchair inside watching television. A squat man with a rounded head and large fiery rounded eyes, his head was balding with galled tufts to its surround.

'I would hold a caution with that girl, she chose to take a bullet to a close friend of hers.' Varman looked away from him. 'He aided in the building of the businesses.' He drew his eyes to the flowering white petals to the table.

'The death was not meant to happen,' he said.

'I was there watching her.' Varman, a tall heavily built man with a full brawny torso, lifted his hand to his brow.

'You were there watching her but you were distracted,' said Harvey.

'I watched them the whole time,' he replied.

'We leave you there running the operation with him and you become involved with her in a side room when you should have been working.' He stared at Varman.

'I would ask that you hold your comments to yourself, I was quite focused,' Varman said nervously.

'Do not speak to me like that.' The large balding man standing in a baggy suit raised a finger to point. 'We left you and trusted you to take care of things and you became distracted with a girl in a side room, allowing the shooting to happen.' He had left Varman at a house to watch over a pair of girls that were witnesses to a shooting. They were able to close down a rival gang with their testimonies in court.

'She was beautiful and very friendly,' Varmen said remembering her.

'You were not meant to take your eyes off the other girl.' Harvey's cheeks reddened as he became angry.

'Why was she so important,' he replied, looking down at his large black boots

'She was aa witness to another attack and would have helped us close them down.' Harvey banged an open hand on the kitchen table. The television was tuned to the racing, and he turned to watch the beginning of the races.

'I wasn't to know that her friend had a gun with her,' said Varman. He shrugged his shoulders.

'What about Harry?' Harvey turned from the television to face him, with his large stumpy hands to his hips.

'He was sent to a man and he made a right mess of it,' said Varman.

'How are we going to sort this mess out?' Harvey replied.

'I can't believe he did it, Harvey.' He pulled at his suit jacket nervously.

'He was meant to get him in the car and shoot him, leaving him parked down a side alley but instead he wasted him the street.' He turned and flung his arms open.

'That sort of business gets us in trouble, Harvey, with the police,' said Varman.

'You can't just kill them in the street,' he replied.

'You should ensure that your own operations are completed.' He gently brushed at his hand across his jacket to straighten the loose sleeve.

'We spoke. I will ensure that the boy that undertook the failed shooting is killed.' His telephone handset rang and he lifted it from the pocket inside of his jacket.

'That is not enough.' He passed the mobile telephone to Harvey who stood beside him. He took the handset and viewed it, understanding the information on the screen.

'The photograph of the shipment,' said Varman sullenly.

'I have seen the shipment,' said Harvey with a frown.

'You said you wanted a photograph.' He reached for his pocket returning the phone.

'We need to know who killed him in the street.' Harvey pointed to his face. 'You are to torture the kid that viewed the killing until he speaks and I wish to be present.' He viewed him through rounded fiery eyes. 'I would not enjoy today to excess, refrain from drinking excessively because I wish to view his murder, errors are a risk to the business.'

'That is fine. Relax and enjoy the races on the television first.' Varman took a seat in an armchair. 'Look, if you wish, Harvey, we will get the kid brought in now from the street and held until we are finished here and this will allow us to speak with him this evening. He has a young girlfriend that we could collect with him.'

'We could have sex with the girl and simultaneously beat the kid to death,' said Harvey gripping his large hands.

'We should wait until tomorrow. I will enjoy the racing on the television. I am enjoying the highlights and then you will bring him to me.' Harvey took his seat beside Varman.

'We will understand the reasoning behind the mistake. Don't worry too much,' Varman said.

Harvey looked across the room at his betting sheet that he had left on the table beside the chair. He felt a little guilty but he had chosen not to go to golf, so he could watch the horses race instead.

'What would you like to do after lunch?' said Harvey. 'After the race has finished, we can take a walk across town.' Harvey settled back down for the race. They had gotten annoyed, waiting for Stephanie to arrive so had put two lots of food onto a plate and left it in the oven.

'Would you try to telephone her again please, Varman, I am annoyed that she hasn't turned up and you have put a great deal of time and effort into that food.' He looked towards the television and didn't move his eyes from the screen, the races had started and the horses were in the paddock. A horse dressed in a pink rug was being led around the ring. Harvey had placed his money on the horse to win.

'There is no one answering. I am sure that she is fine, she is with that new guy.' He stood up from his chair and grasped a tea towel. He flicked the tea towel over his shoulder and rolled his eyes before returning to the sink. At the sink, he began to lather up the roasting pan and then left it on the side to soak.

'I am not keen on the new guy,' said Harvey.

'If he has an arrogant manner, then you have to remember that you have achieved far more than he has Harvey,' said Varman calming him.

'I just worry about who she is with,' Harvey said.

'I would not worry too much, they are old enough to look after themselves and we are here if there is any trouble,' he replied. Harvey picked up his paper, folded it into four, and with his biro, readied himself for the race.

The last horses were leaving the enclosure and were being brought out onto the track and into the stiles. Just then the front door flung open and in walked Janine.

'What time do you call this.' He dropped his paper down to his knees in disbelief that they had arrived just as the race was about to begin. 'You have delayed dinner,' he said, quickly gesturing for her to move out of the way of the screen with a wave of his paper so that he could begin to watch the races.

'I am sorry that I am late,' she said, ignoring him.

'Move Janine,' he said looking over his glasses. She slumped herself down on the arm of his chair.

'What are you watching?' she said. She loved her father, she sat on the arm and put her arm around him. He would usually be very happy with the attention from her, he hardly ever saw her since she had begun her new relationship, but now was not the time to be interrupting him.

'I am watching the races, Janine, they are about to begin,' he said grandly and sat back in the arm chair. 'Get off the arm of the chair, you will break it, sit in that seat.' He tapped her leg with the paper and gave her a gentle nudge with his elbow. She stood, walked across to the chair opposite, where Varman would usually sit and slumped into it.

'Are you OK, Varman? I am knackered.' She was tired from her night out. She sat in tight jeans and a jacke,t her bleached-blonde hair rested on her back. He had kept her up all night. She looked across to Varman at the smell of food.

'Where is he?' said Harvey as Varman put her plate of food into the microwave with the second plate covered, and waiting to go in, on the side.

'Where's who?' she said dryly. 'You mean Mark? I thought that I told you we aren't together any more. I met a new guy, he is nice.'

'If they ever say anything to you, we want to know, Janine,' said Harvey.

'We will have them sorted out,' replied Varman. Varman placed the dinner onto the table and picked up the second plate. 'You should have brought the new guy with you I have a dinner saved here for him.'

'He is with me but he is not coming in here with you pair,' she replied gazing at the screen.

'So come and eat your dinner and tell us all about your new fella,' Said Varman, pulling back the seat at the table.

'He is in the car, I only popped in, to say hello. I am not staying,' she said, with her car keys jangling in her hand.

'I have just reheated your dinner, go and get him and bring him in,' said Varman.

'No way, I have only just met the fella, he would be scared to death if I bought him in here to meet with you two. I am going to go after eating this.'

She stood up and hovered for a while playing with her keys and waiting for her father to look up from the television. She dropped her shoulders a little when he didn't and leant over and tapped him on the shoulder with the key in her hand.

'What, Janine, I am watching the race, now sit down and eat I will talk to you afterwards,' he said without looking away from the television. He tapped his leg as the horses were released from the stiles and he leant forward in his chair, getting closer and closer to the television.

'I am going to have to go and get him from the car,' said Janine standing up and beginning to pass in front of the television.

'Out of the way, Janine,' he said, leaning forwards and moving her with his hand to one side. He leant further forwards and cheered at the television. 'Go on.' he said looking at the horses and getting more and more excited as the race progressed.

Janine looked at the television and then back at her father and stood motionless, frowning in bewilderment at his excitement.

'He will have to wait in the car, your dinner is ready, sit and have your dinner and then be on your way,' said Harvey over his shoulder. Her father stood from the chair and began to shout at the television.

'How much have you got on this Dad?' She thought that he must have a lot of money riding on this race.

'I hold relations with a new partner,' she said as he stood before the television.

'Did you hear that she has found a new fella,' said Varmen.

'I heard. What does he work as?' he said, pretending to care. The horses were nearing the line and his horse was just about to win by a head. 'Go on,' he shouted. 'Over you go.' He raised his hands into the air and began to jump on the spot, his belly began to wobble in front of him through his suit jacket. He began to cheer and tears formed in his eyes.

Chapter 18
Aston

A tall, fair-faced man with a head of brilliant white hair, his large round eyes were piercing blue and his nose was large. He wore a uniform of stiff blue suit with a white shirt beneath, a firm handkerchief adorned his pocket. He carried a suitcase. His long saloon vehicle stood stationary at the front of the church with the motor on.

'Good morning, could you show me to the cafe.' He gave an address card to a young man standing at the roadside. He wore blue jeans and a loose shirt.

'The cafe is right there on the corner.' The man raised his hand and pointed to the corner of the street.

'I will walk along there now, thank you for the directions.' He passed along the street to find a cafe with a large covered terrace with tables and umbrellas. He took a seat in a quiet corner and upon seeing Denem and Kirsten arrive, he lifted a large hand to get his attention.

'Good morning, Denem,' he said waving. 'Good morning, Kirsten.'

'Good morning Suliam you arrived early.' He walked to the table and pulled out his chair.

Kirsten's straight, black hair, fell across her oval face and rested on her neck. She brushed her hands down her tight black wool dress.

'We are keen to have this meeting,' Suliam said. 'Please take a seat.'

'We will enjoy the coffee here today it is very good.' Kirsten replied.

'Could we have coffees for the table?' Suliam said to the waiter. A thin man made a note of the order.

'I walked through the streets to the café, the car dropped me a number of blocks back.' Suliam pointed across his shoulder. They both turned.

'There is an interesting shopping mall that sits beside the church,' said Denem.

'It is newly built and is filled with the newest shops' Kirsten added.

'I saw the shopping mall, I passed beside it this morning,' Suliam said.

'It is one of ours, we built it as part of an investment plan.' Denem touched the lapel of his jacket, revealing a gold timepiece.

'There are many new buildings in that part of the city,' Suliam said. The man's large, blue eyes, rested upon them both.

'Here is the coffee,' said Denem. The waiter placed three steaming cups on the table.

'Thank you,' Kirsten said.

'Do you take sugar?' Denem pushed the sugar bowl.

'I enjoy sugar I will also take one of those biscotti,' said Kirsten.

'Go for it there are plenty of them,' said Suliam. Denem had attended the meeting today with his aide. He knew that this would be one of the final chances to gain the script from Suliam. He had to convince him today. A young pair stood from a table opposite, and knowing Denem, began to speak to him. The girl's summer dress flowed and her long thin legs had low boots on.

'You are taking a coffee together, that's nice,' said the girl.

'It's good to see you here,' replied Denem.

'I haven't seen you recently where have you been?' said the man.

'I have been close with a girl, so I have spent much of my time with her,' Denem said.

'We could get together again, it has been so long.' She raised a hand to stop her skirt lifting.

'I will arrange an evening at the house and invite you and your husband along.' Denem smiled.

'We are to visit Katrina's home this evening for dinner, I considered purchasing a new dress for the occasion,' said the girl taking a step closer.

'There are boutiques at the edge of the city that have many dresses that may be suitable,' said Kirsten.

'We could stop there on our drive home and take a look.' The girl looked at the man beside her and raised her hand to his arm.

'Bye for now,' said Kirsten and the couple moved away.

'Sorry about that, we have known each other for many years,' said Denem.

'That's fine.' Suliam collected his coffee. 'We have got a lot to talk about today.'

'We are to talk about the new waterfront developments,' said Denem thinking about the script.

'The towers in the sea,' said Kirsten excitedly.

'They are not really in the sea but they do appear that way,' said Denem with a frown.

'They are built upon islands, we know this,' said Kirsten.

'We viewed the photographs, they will look spectacular,' said Suliam, viewing Kirsten's dark hair.

'Most people are very happy with the plans,' said Denem

'I am really glad that I invested,' said Suliam, resting a large hand on the table. His suitcase stood beside him.

'These should be good when they complete,' said Denem

'When will we be able to visit them,' said Suliam. They looked at his large blue eyes.

'We are able to visit now to view them being constructed,' said Kirsten.

'We could go down there next week and take a look at them,' said Denem, raising his hand to point.

'I am very happy with the way that things are going,' said Suliam.

'Could you tell us, about your business, you are sometimes difficult to get hold of,' said Denem.

'I work as an investor but there is increasing work with the armed forces.' He tilted his large head and smirked.

'What work do you mean?' Kirsten said viewing to his white hair and his large face.

'We take work that is high profile,' he replied.

'What do you mean by high profile,' she said.

'We make resolve on countries that are attacking our own,' said Suliam with defiance. He furrowed his brow, sitting back in his chair.

'Are you in the field?' Denem said.

'I am mainly remote and undertake tasks through a switchboard,' Suliam replied. A waiter returned to the table and added more milk.

'Is the tasking from a building in the city?' said Denem.

'Yes, I work from a switchboard in the city and it allows me to see everything that I need to see through satellite links,' Suliam said looking at Denem's hair, parted to the side.

'You are able to monitor large areas,' Denem said.

'We monitor and then we are also assigned work.' He

thought back to his assignments. He focused upon the map in the plastic slip that hung around his neck. He rolled over, and lifting the document up, he shone a torch onto it. He wanted to understand his positioning. There had been gunfire close beside him. He had managed to avoid the militia that had passed him in a convoy of vehicles and the concrete pipe had allowed him the cover.

'I want to talk about all of the other work that we are doing with you,' said Denem.

'In addition to the investments you mean,' Suliam replied.

'Yes, in addition to them,' said Denem.

'We are happy with the investments and we would now like to offer you the script,' said Suliam. His laurel green eyes resting firmly upon the table.

'That is great news,' said Denem, excitedly.

'The script will allow you access the bank vault,' said Suliam.

'That is all that I wanted.' Denem touched his dark solemn hair.

'We have everything that we require from you so we are content to sell the script,' said Suliam.

'When will we finalise,' said Denem.

'We will finalise today.' Suliam moved to collect his suitcase from beside him.

'So am I able to take the script from you now?' said Denem.

'There it is, everything that you require.' Suliam lifted up a flap in his suitcase and retrieved a disc that he placed onto the table. Denem placed his large hand on top of it.

'That is fine.' Denem smirked. 'Shall we order more coffee?'

'Could we get more coffee over here please?' said Suliam, shouting over his shoulder.

'Did I tell you about my new horses?' said Denem.

'No, you didn't,' he replied.

'I recently purchased a number of new horses for my livery.' Denem straightened the sleeve of his jacket.

'They are something that I would be keen to see,' said Suliam leaning into the table.

'You are welcome to visit and view them,' said Denem.

'How was it, purchasing them?' said Suliam.

'I initially had problems with the purchase of them, a gentlemen let me down but that problem became resolved,' he said.

'What happened?' said Suliam.

'He promised me a steed and then didn't sell.' Denem raised a large hand to rest on the table.

'It happens sometimes,' Suliam replied.

'I have the stables ready for visitors they keep them especially tidy,' said Denem.

'I will most definitely visit.' He viewed Kirsten's black hair resting neatly on her neck. 'We could eat dinner on that occassion.'

'We will also arrange for dinner,' said Denem.

'We could visit at the end of next month,' Suliam said.

'That sounds just fine,' said Denem with a grin. He lifted his arm, with a blue blazer sleeve held closed with gold buttons, and he pointed a long finger. 'Would you want to ride some of the horses?'

'I have ridden before but it was a long time ago,' Suliam replied smirking.

'If you feel up for it, we could take the horses out,' said Denem, eager to impress the man.

'Where will we go?' said Suliam.

'We could ride across the fields close to my home,' said Denem.

'That sounds fun,' he replied.

As Denem put the disc from the table into the inside of his jacket, Suliam thought again about his work. Suliam stared at him, and knocked his hand away and the man slumped to the floor at his feet. He reached for a gun and with a loud bang the man lay on his side, still. He reached for the slip of paper content, with the current state of the country's wealth. Suliam returned his attention to Denem.

'When you visit, will you bring your wife with you?' said Denem.

'My wife is a ballerina,' he replied, lifting his large head proudly.

'A ballernia?' Denem replied, impressed.

'She is currently in a production with the royal ballet,' said Suliam.

'She must work very hard,' said Denem.

'She has trained all of her life since she was a small girl and has achieved a great deal,' said Suliam.

'She is welcome to visit with you,' said Denem touching his dark brown hair.

'She may be under a training regime that will not allow for the leisure time, but I will ask her,' he replied, checking his watch.

'Is her current production selling out?' said Denem.

'They are selling all of their tickets most evenings.' Suliam sat back in his chair. A group of people beside them got up to leave.

'When she has free time we must get together,' said Denem, touching the lapel of his jacket.

'You could visit a performance with your partner,' said Suliam.

'I would like that very much,' Denem said.

'We will arrange for tickets to be sent across to you,' said Suliam, his blue eyes upon Denem.

'What a treat that will be.' Denem crossed his arms.

'My wife was hit with injury some years back and we spent our time visiting a number of countries,' said Suliam lowering the suitcase back to the floor.

'That sounds fun.' Denem passed him a smile. 'I hope that she has made a full recovery.'

'She made a full recovery and now she is performing to her very best,' said Suliam.

'What countries did you visit?' said Denem, looking at Kirsten and smiling.

'We visited South American countries,' Suliam replied

'Did you travel very far, or were you main stream?' said Denem, raising a hand to rest on the table.

'We stayed within the cities, we did venture to view archaeological remains on a number of occasions,' said Suliam. A table beside laughed.

'There are great attractions in the hillsides,' said Denem, lifting a sleeve to check his watch.

'We walked for many miles to view the remains,' said Suliam.

'There are whole cities below the ground,' Denem said eagerly.

'The cities are worth viewing too, they are staggering in their expanse,' said the tall, fair-faced man with a head of brilliant white hair.

'I would enjoy viewing the remains very much but it is just

finding the time to go,' said Denem.

'Shall we meet again a different day?' Suliam replied, gazing across the cafe to the door.

'We could meet again and we should stay in touch now that our business is settled,' said Denem.

'We will remain close,' Suliam replied, reassuringly.

Chapter 19
Jordie

The brightly lit square before her had turning fairground rides filled with children. The rows of horses were finely carved with brightly painted flowers and sea urchins that covered the bodies of the striding creatures. The canopy above the horses was stripy red with a small flag that flapped and waved above in the wind. Those surrounding the ride stood closely huddled together in hats and scarves. They watched the winding horses as they heaved up and down on their rockers with people seated on them and with their arms grabbing the air before onlookers. Stephanie's curly brown hair fell to the sides of her face resting on her cheeks. She carried with her a soft leather bag with rigid upright handles. She took large strides that carried her through the crowd of excited people. She walked between people with her chin raised high above the crowd, finding Denem standing before the horse carousel.

'We will go to the carousel and take a horse together.' He looked at her with his green eyes raising his hand to the ride.

'We are lucky that we found each other, I thought that we would have to look for each other everywhere in this crowded square.'

'We are together now and that is what counts,' he said, reassuringly.

'You are looking good. You are amazing do you know that?' she said, resting her hand on his jacket.

'It's great to be here with you, it's overwhelming how I feel,' he said, smirking shyly.

'When a person is overwhelmed, is that good or bad?' she demanded. Her curly brown hair resting on her cheeks.

'It's good if you are in control of yourself.'

'I am in control, I know what I want. I want you.' She rested a pointed finger on him.

'I want you to.' He grinned at her. 'We haven't been together for a while. How was Dan?'

'He was fine. I missed you though.'

'What did you do together, you were there for some time? I expected you back,' Denem replied.

'We held a dinner with guests,' she said excitedly.

'There are sweets there if you want them.' He pointed to the jars of sweets on the shelf of a stand. His eyes passing her, followed the horses spinning on the carousel that were painted with bright flowers, scaly fish and the creatures of the sea.

'We should ride the carousel together.' She titled her head eagerly to view him with her eyes widening.

'Yes, we will find ourselves a horse right now,' Denem replied, as they passed beside of a group of girls standing close to the ride. They took the final few steps up onto the riding platform.

'I have got everything that I want but I still desire something more from you,' she said softly, as he helped her to the horse they were to ride together. She reached forwards and tenderly touched to his pale hands.

'I only want you beside me on this ride, and through life.' He straddled the ride and she moved her arms before her and leaning back, she rested her head against his shoulder as he spooned her.

'When we are riding so closely together there is a good

feeling that comes from you,' she said faintly.

'I like being close to you, it's comforting.' He gazed at her heavy brown loose hair falling in curls across the strong structure of her long face as the ride turned.

'It is good that you feel that way. You really are becoming close to me.'

The ride circled and from the height of the horse, she viewed across the crowds. She clasped his waist feeling shielded and calm in his company. 'We are heading for something more in our partnership.' She loved him dearly and she had followed by his side for many months, to become part of his dreams. He aimed to gain something more through his investments and to uncover the script. She wanted more charge from him now. If she was to keep him beside her he would have to commit to her. She was initially concerned with the challenges that she faced each day through her meetings with other men that he had arranged for her, but she had found in herself, a new confidence.

As the carousel completed its circle, Stephanie found herself before the steps of the ride. He turned to her and she reached forwards to kiss him on his sturdy cheek, resting her hand on his supple shirt tucked beneath his coat. To steady herself she touched his hard body with her finger tips. He viewed her pale smooth skin with lines to either side of her shapely mouth. Her large rounded piercing blue eyes fluttered at him from deep within the frame of her face. He viewed her cheeks and nose as she lowered her long bony chin.

'We have got far to go together before we get to the point that you want to be at with your life.'

He smirked charmingly. 'I am happy with you like this. The script will be revealed and the meetings can then stop.' She was attending meetings for him with men and Dan was one of the men that she was meeting with.

'I am able to make more for us both living with you,' she said, as she moved her hand to the front of his chin, touching the stubble on his face. 'The hands of the man upon me are only of meaning when they are yours.'

'It is meaningful when we are together.'

'We did not understand how much more we would understand ourselves, we are becoming a serious couple.' She gazed at him earnestly. 'You are only able to find yourself with me.'

'I find myself with many people, they are people from everywhere but I do feel something special for you.' They passed beside a large hammer and scales which tested how hard they could hit the pad. They passed golden tokens for the slot of the measuring device and clambered to grab the large hammer.

'I will make our love stronger, I promise you that.' She touched his arm, giggling.

'Let's talk about this more later, we are going somewhere with this and it is you and me together. That is what we both want,' Denem replied, viewing her. She began to clamber from the hammer and scales and he flung the hammer down at the pad, causing the bell to ring.

'You hit that well Denem,' she said.

'We are together but our work is so challenging,' he replied. She tilted her head gazing at him. 'I understand that it is diifficut for you meeting with the men.'

'You are so hard on us, we are in love, Denem, that is why we are together today. Forget about them.'

'I am able to give you commitment, I know that is what you want.' He stood in a long green coat with a white shirt released over his lean torso. She began to make her way along the platform to the steps. Girls sat holding pink candyfloss on sticks, their faces were covered with the pink sticky mess.

Denem walked beside her as they passed the steps of the carousel once more. He raised his pale hand to rest on her thin waist. She took slow steps beside the riding platform, losing her footing she reached for his hand with her own.

'These were the hands that caught your attention when we were sitting together for the first time,' she spoke looking up to him as he grasped her. She turned her head away from him, the chin of her long face lifted high, her full distinct heavy dark brown hair rested beyond her shoulders in loose curls.

'These were the arms of strength that collected us into that deep embrace.' He raised both of his sturdy pale hands, placing them upon her.

'There is more for us both with the gentle touch of our hands across each other.' Gazing at him, she moved her hands slowly across his, touching his supple skin with her fingertips.

'I enjoy your touch,' he said softly.

'That is why I like you, I want for more from you,' she replied.

'I will give you more,' he promised. Looking around him he saw her friends seated on a bench. 'We could go over there and visit these girls, aren't they your friends?' He pointed with his arm outstretched to a group of girls that sat on a wooden bench to the far side of the square.

'I called them and asked them to meet us here. I told them we were going to the fair.' The girls held giant lollipops in their hands, that they licked at.

'I recognised them. These are your friends that we met with before, Stephanie, together we will all go somewhere after here.'

'There are always good people that want to meet with us and

these are my dear friends.'

'It is good to meet you all, are we going to your house from here?' Jordie asked. She sat frowning with a blonde bob of hair. She collected her hands to her flat chest before her with her mouth held wide open waiting for his response.

'We all might go to the house,' Stephanie replied.

'There are likely to be many more people that you are able to meet at the property,' Denem said viewing the fair-haired girl before him. She smirked through straight teeth to him as she sat on the bench beside her friend.

'She could come with me if you want,' she said, pointing to Jamie. He nodded in agreeance and waved his hand for them to move along to allow Stephanie to take a seat.

Denem seated, smiled at the carousel as it began to pass, the music louder, before filling with people and beginning to slowly turn. The carousel turned and the riders on the gracefully painted white horses began to wave their hands to those standing in the square. Many stood crowded by the counters filled with soft toys and lollipops. The tents were brightly lit with generous men standing in aprons filled with money and collecting the golden tokens. Jordie passed a look across her shoulder to Denem with a shy pout from red lips. Her back turned, and with her head positioned away from him, she moved her hair allowing it to tumble and fall down her back in curls, before she stood and began striding away from the bench of girls with Stephanie smirking at her. She took grand strides back to the ride. As she walked, she spoke, 'Look, I elevate my legs, knees and feet as I walk, it is as if I am a horse cantering as I prance to the platform.'

'You do not appear like a horse,' Jamie, her friend, replied.

'Well, I could look more like a horse if I wanted to.'

'I shall spur you on,' Stephanie spoke with a squeal. 'A

crowd raised, you whip up excitement.'

She raised a skeletal hand to her friend as she spun to return to them with a large smirk across her face, her lips shapely and accentuated. Her thumbs held onto her belt as she stopped a distance from them to pose.

'You are a horse on this occasion.' Denem stood and walked beside her, gazing at the carousel. 'Do not harness yourself, release to the movement of your body.' He viewed her slender body and down to her feet on the floor. She made the sound of a horse to him with her lips puffing with air as she stamped her feet. He raised both of his sturdy pale hands and began to patter at them.

'I am a horse,' she said as she did a little skip. She reached the seat with her friends seated on it and they all began to giggle as they watched her. Stephanie pretended to hold the reins of a horse in front of her. They all began to giggle. Jamie was a runner that exercised in pink tracksuit around her block. Clutching a brightly coloured water carrier and with neon sweatbands on her forehead and wrists she would run the local neighbourhood. She grew up with a family of health-conscious parents. Her mother would collect berries and fruits from the garden whilst her father would pluck beans and dig potatoes from a rich allotment patch.

'Be horses with pace and style in front of me to my home. Let us go there now, there is a car waiting.' Denem raised his arm to cup his large burnished hand to his ear to listen for an answer from them and the two tall girls beside Stephanie immediately stood, excited to leave with them. The sound of the music from the carousel began fading as they strode away from the large fairground ride.

'We are not with you both because of your money you know,' said Jordie.

'Money is not everything, I meet with nice people that hold small amounts of money and they are always warm-hearted,' Denem spoke as he overheard her.

'They are going to enjoy themselves with us aren't you girls,' Stephanie chose to say as she passed before them, both linking his arm as they approached the large black car. The door to the car was held open by a man in casual clothing, a hooded top and a large jacket over it. The seat of the car was soft, pale leather. Jamie reached the car seat, and leaning over, she threw her handbag a distance from herself on the leather, and it slid to rest against the hard panel of the far door. She then clambered into the car with a tug of her skirt to cover her thighs. She had known Jordie for many years, she remembered her when she lived in the city as a child brought up in a small apartment with her mother, their father had left them alone to fend for themselves. Jordie's mother was also a dancer and model, she had attended dance school each day after her schooling just as she had chosen for her daughter.

'I have got so many tokens left over.' Her friend Jordie took her seat clutching golden tokens clumsily with her finely painted nails.

'I was winning more than you and all of mine have gone. We had such a good time.' Jamie spoke through straight white teeth as her friend shuffled over the soft leather of the car seat.

'I am in the front here beside the driver, you guys count your tickets in the back.' Stephanie walked to the front of the vehicle that had white paint, and large, silver shiny wheels.

'We are going to a house a short distance from here,' Denem said, shutting the door. 'We are to drive there and to relax at my place for the evening.'

'There are many that want his company we are lucky,'

Stephanie replied, giving him a push with her finger as she climbed into the front seat opposite the girls.

'Come on, Denem, get in.' Jamie leant forwards, and pulling her skirt across her knees, she lurched forwards to find him as he looked at the driver, passing him a wink, before sitting beside the two girls in the back seat, crossing his legs before him. He wore finely pressed trousers of the softest material, his shoes long and shiny.

'Stephanie we are going to a meeting tomorrow at the house with people,' he said as the car began to pull away. Denem viewed her, raising both of his sturdy, pale hands. 'We are finalising discussions with regard to a number of investments.'

'They like to talk as they eat. We should have them prepare the table for us to eat in the large room at the front of the house,' she said. Her heavy, brown loose hair falling in curls across the strong structure of her long face.

'That could be a good idea, we'll seat them all there.'

'A friend of mine should attend, Jordie will go. I can't be there, she will be good for you instead of me,' Stephanie replied. She turned her head proudly away from him, the chin of her long face lifted high.

'Why can't you be there, they will want for you to be with them.'

'I've got to go to a friend's party, it is a girl that you know well, she is a close friend of Dan Hayworth.' She viewed his angular face from her blue eyes. 'Jordie will happily attend instead of me.'

'That sounds fine, get her to come along.' He viewed across to Jordie seated beside him. 'Are you OK with that, Jordie?'

'Should be a smash,' she replied, smirking with her fists clenched to her lap.

'I am going to the party at the house, they are visiting with dresses for us to wear,' she said looking at one of the girls opposite. 'I like that hairclip that you are wearing.' Stephanie leant forwards, ignoring Denem, and touched the fingertips of her hand to her blonde hair that hadthe red bow. The girl lifted to her hand and their hands touched and she grinned at her, opening her legs as she relaxed in her company.

'I am looking forward to visiting here with you both,' said Jordie.

Denem seated beside them, touched her bare thighs and she opened her legs further. 'We are to be together for the evening, I might wear that bow myself later.' She pulled it from her hair.

Chapter 20
Issy

Stephanie strode to the fireplace, and with her hand, touched the ornate white surround. Decorative rope twisted between the faces and passed the shelf, wrapping it with painted blue bells and golden leaves. She viewed Denem, wearing a fine white shirt with wide trousers and thin leather belt. He grasped her with large pale hands and cupping his hands to her head pulled at her to kiss her lips. Stephanie, angry with bright blue eyes, stared at Issy seated on the carpet covered with woven leaves upon the walnut floor.

'There are two of us here, Denem, you should choose which one you want. We may not be here tomorrow,' she spoke aggressively. She lifted her arms from her sides linking them around Denem's neck, with her fine bony hands.

'When we do not occupy the present, we are left without ourselves,' he said contemplating.

'Why do we need anybody but the two of us, Denem,' said Stephanie.

'It is beauty that occupies our thoughts in moments like this, with you both there beside me.'

'He is saying that he has beauty, not you,' Issy said doubtfully.

'He does not mean you either, if he's saying that.'

Issy remembered how beautiful she was. She marched through the door looking with her blue eyes to the man seated in the deep armchair at the large oak table. It was her first time visiting the offices. He passed her a hand to dismiss her and she stood before him and hitched up her short skirt. He grinned and standing from the desk, he removed his glasses, settling them on a glossy magazine resting open in front of him. He asked her to undress and a lengthy photoshoot ensued.

Denem lifted his hands to release to her black leather bodice, shedding it on the floor. She stood in heeled snakeskin shoes, her warm skin bare to the lit fire. The flames writhing in the fireplace, that was covered with gold emblems on the grille. She passed her elegant hand across his body and he took a stride from her with green beguiling eyes to Stephanie.

'Join me here upon the carpet and allow us to lay together.' Issy excitedly moved her hand over the entwined carpet with flowers and verdure. They ignored her and continued to gaze at each other.

'Plotting and scheming against me is not allowed,' said Stephanie pointing to his bare chest.

'We can make plans together rather than feel that way,' he said smirking.

'I will scheme for our love, Denem.' She gazed at him.

'I want lots of good thoughts and I will help make those thoughts with you,' he replied.

'We are plotting and scheming together right now,' she said defiantly and feeling a little happier in herself with Issy being there. A lamp stood tall upon a thin silver stand, above a set of low seaters. Large plants held white clay pots with leaves twisting to the branches.

'We will lay with Issy upon the carpet, collect a number of cushions,' he growled enjoying her appearance as she lounged on the soft carpet. Stephanie, reluctant, viewed her and then slowly moved to grasp the large silk cushions.

'I wish her to go, she is sitting there all prissy, brushing her hair.' She became angry as she turned to her. 'You are not beautiful you should leave.'

'Lay the cushions on the carpet. Collect more for us,' he hollered.

'I am holding them, Denem, there is enough here,' said Stephanie, slyly viewing the thin woman seated on the carpet. 'We are forced to join to you, Issy.'

Stephanie hesitantly threw the cushions on the floor. Issy, kneeling, passed the fingertips of her hands through the curls of her long mousey blonde hair. Stephanie, grasping another cushion threw it towards her, in her anger, knocking a jug of water across the side table that began to run and pool on the floor.

Issy leant forwards and passed her elbows to the cushions and small white feathers filled the air. The feathers floated, resting on the patterned carpet. Stephanie blew at them and waved her graceful hands to move them.

'Don't stand there alone, join to us both here. The feathers are everywhere, roll around with us both down here,' said Issy. Denem viewed the frame of her face, her pointed chin and cheekbones with smirk lines to the sides of her mouth. Her body was thin with long limbs. Stephanie sat on the cushions beside her with her legs bent in front of her and began with her hands to part Issy's long hair.

'What makes a good moment,' said Stephanie with a silky tone.

'Fun and excitement makes a good moment,' Issy replied as she touched her hair.

'We are making moments all the time together, moments to remember,' Stephanie replied whispering in her ear as she parted her hair.

'I am a fun person and so are you,' said Issy, grasping a red ribbon in her hand and passing it over her shoulder, to Stephanie behind her. 'When we are fun we make those moments.'

Denem passed his large pale hands to gently touch Issy's hair, joining Stephanie.

'Stephanie, collect fruit from the table and ask that they collect jugs of water to replace those.' Stephanie collected a silver tray of apples and red garden berries to the heavy weave carpet for eating. 'When you have finished with her hair then apply her make-up,' he said. He watched as Stephanie's hips rocked as she moved in a stately manner across the room before Issy in a black, heeled shoe.

'He wants me to take care of you.' She slowly kneeled on her bony legs to collect to Issy's blonde hair into bundles with her hands.

'Thank you for helping me with my hair, Stephanie,' she said. Issy gracefully lifted a berry between fingertips to her mouth and then pointed to a glass that held deep red wine. Stephanie, with a sigh, reluctantly collected the glass and passed it to her.

'You were saying that you visited to buy clothes,' Stephanie asked.

'I collected a couple of pairs of new shoes and a raincoat.' Issy excitedly viewed her through blue, oval eyes.

'Where are they I will take a look at them,' said Stephanie and Issy pointed a hand towards bags that she had collected with her, beside the low seater.

'They are in the designer bags right there. Take the coat from the wrapping if you want.'

Stephanie held in her hands red ribbons that she began to tie to Issy's hair, her hair rested in plaits over her shoulders.

'What arouses you, and you can't just say me,' said Denem moving closer to them on the carpet.

'I want someone that understands my needs and requirements,' said Stephanie, defiantly.

'How do I know what they are if you do not tell me,' he replied.

'I will teach you and you can teach me, we will learn from each other,' she said reaching out to him with an open hand and touching his leg.

'I am enjoying being here with you both today,' said Denem

'She is spoiling it,' said Stephanie slyly.

'I am not spoiling anything, get away from him I want him to myself,' Issy replied laughing, her blonde hair wispy on her face and across her cheeks, she began to blow at it away with thin, red lips.

'I want him, take your hands from him, Issy,' Stephanie replied.

'There is plenty here for you both.' He lifted his strong pale hands to the two girls and begun to wrap his arms around Issy.

Stephanie distractedly viewed a large crystal stone chandelier hung central in the room that soared with brightly coloured sparkling jewels. She viewed the corner of the room, an ornate golden cage holding a large parrot that gave out a giant squawk.

'You are to take to drinks from the cabinet,' Denem growled, as he bite into an apple from the heavy silver tray.

'We are sitting here, Denem, she will make us something special,' said Issy with a wild tone. Issy collected the soft silk cushions closer to her, patting at them to invite Denem closer. As she did, she remembered another dear friend of hers and how they had met. The man began to whimper and she froze. She had been writing her report for the newspaper for several hours. They sat together reporting behind separate computers. She heard him whimper again and then, with a gasp of air, he began to sob. He lowered his head and she walked over to him, wrapping her arms around him to console him. The man's wife had committed suicide. She became his dear friend and confidante.

'Cherries are better than apples, you should eat cherries with me.' Denem viewed two martini glasses filled with red liquid to a heavy silver tray, with a tumbler of golden whisky.

'I enjoy shiny ripe red cherries,' said Issy.

'I visited cherry blossom trees filled with white petals, it is beautiful when the trees are together, they create a white canopy,' Denem said.

'We should visit the blossom Denem,' Issy said excitedly. He collected his heavy crystal glass to rest on the surface.

Issy collected a martini glass and began sipping at the drink, a shiny cherry revealed in its base. She took the cherry to her mouth and positioned it between her straight white teeth. She then bit slowly into the fruit. 'Kiss me.' Issy moved forwards and touched Stephanie's mouth to hers and they began to enjoy the cherry together.

'Have we found love,' said Denem to the two girls, as they finally began to enjoy each other's company.

'Love does render us closer together and we are together right now,' said Stephanie, breaking from her kiss to gaze at Denem.

'We've always been together,' he replied.

'We've always been together but it hasn't been like this, I want trust,' she said, longingly.

'Trust is so difficult, you become hurt so easily,' Denem said, thoughtfully.

'We have to trust to find love,' Stephanie replied, her tone dying. She wanted love from this man but he invited too many women into their lives. She wanted him for herself and she couldn't have him. She was becoming disgruntled and was considering leaving him to return to be with Dan, her previous boyfriend. She had speant months with Dan and had grown to like him again. Issy was his final curse.

Issy, wearing a silk sheen bodice tied tight across her ribs, her cheeks like red paint, her lips thin and her eyes in a line of black make-up gazed at Denem.

'At the event that you are planning will there be a person that specialises in jewels.' Stephanie passed him a look through a bony face held with blue rounded eyes gazing at his hair, parted to the side above his angular face.

'Diamonds are shipped with other stones from the continent,' Denem growled. Issy took a sip of her wine and lipstick printed from her thin lips onto the heavy cut glass. 'I hold stones, what do you want to look at, do you have a favourite to view?'

An inquisitive frown became strewn upon Stephanie's face with prominent nose and cheekbones proud to the pointed cage of her face.

'Why do stones pass that route,' she asked loudly with a breath. She viewed him through eyes run with black make-up from their encounter. He lifted a large hand to her with a handkerchief, exhaling she grasped at it on her face.

'The stones travel through the Pacific where they are purchased by business people that visit the ocean's islands. They are cut there and distributed. One takes hold of a large diamond stone.' He lifted his hand to rest on the pocket of his sumptuous black textured jacket. 'You will hold the diamond in my pocket later in the evening if you are lucky,' he said teasing them. He viewed the oak panelled walls with a row of paintings at distant blur held in ornate gold frames. 'Diamonds,' he said.

'I viewed your diamonds already, show me this one now, allow me a glimpse.' Issy stood, and passing him, began to stamp her bare feet. He took the stone from his pocket in a velvet bag and he dropped the jewel into the centre of his open hand. He took a breath of air and began to slowly uncurl his large fingers revealing the glimmering object. They all stared to the shimmering diamond.

'I will take that diamond,' said Issy.

Issy remembered someone stealing something from her as she said it. She was sitting in the small cafe writing on her reporting pad. They had visited all of the boutiques and she had many shopping bags with her. Her camera held on her side on a chain that she had linked over the back of her seat. As she collected her glass closer to her, a man appeared before the table and grasped the camera, tearing it from her grip. He ran along the street only to be halted by a driver in a car. Issy sat staring whilst Stephanie pranced towards him with her hips swaying to the room and with blue rounded eyes, her soft hair, brown, and ruffled down her back.

'Denem, we'll go take a seat there and look at the diamond together.' She uttered provocatively.

'Let me hold it now Denem.' Issy cupped her fine hands and he threw it into the air for her to catch. She took hold of the glistening stone with a chuckle. Stephanie, embarrassed, returned upon the low seater and leant her elbows, grasping her soft, leather clutch. She collected a mirror in her hands and began to look at herself. She then lifted a piece of dried fruit from a small plate before her and hurled it towards Denem. The fruit caught on his shirt. Brushing it away with his hand, it fell to the floor. He leant forwards took one from the tray himself, and returned fire.

Chapter 21
Suliam

The large table had been laid with food and they began collecting around it. A great many plates stood with a large browned chicken and bright green and yellow vegetables beside fish with steaming molluscs and shells. Pink cakes and sweets stood tiered on high stands. A tall vase of flowers centred the table above the white tablecloth. Silver knives and forks lay beside large serving spoons that glistened and shone in the light from the chandelier above.

'We are enjoying the delights of the garden,' he said, pointing to a large bowl of fruit and berries.

'There is a fish beside you filled with caviar that we began earlier, take the fish and enjoy some with me. Enjoy the small eggs as they pass into your mouth,' Issy said, bringing herself to the table wearing a tight dress on her thin body. The soft material cut low to her neck revealing her small chest. 'We are enjoying the sea instead of the garden,' she shouted.

'There are more places to visit in our minds than the sea and the garden. We should consider others and be grateful for our food.' Denem spoke softly as he passed beside her, collecting her arm to his and pulling her close to him at the table edge. He collected a golden green grape that he held firmly between two fingers that he placed into his mouth.

'The sea reminds me of home, my sister, and I grew up beside the sea.' He turned to view Issy through his green eyes.

'You should invite your sister to the house. I would like to meet with her.'

He wrapped his arms around her waist, and she gazed up at him touching his angular face. Issy had been visiting the home of Denem for several months and she wanted their relationship to become something more. Stephanie had left and gone to Dan's.

'In the future will we be the same as we are now, do you think,' he said lazily. Keeping her happy, but considering Stephanie.

'We will grow and change and we might become a little more like each other,' Issy said, excitedly.

'I don't want to change,' he replied, coldly.

'We'll change together and the things that we find different we'll enjoy together, we'll enjoy the differences,' she said.

'We'll enjoy the differences, like you might like eating chocolate and I like peanut butter,' he replied. She smirked with large dimples arising on either side of her face. He pointed at Issy and collected her to his arms. He thought of Stephanie.

'I want someone that cares for me, Denem,' she said.

'They are to be gentle and thoughtful,' he replied sharply.

'It is not difficult to find someone that is gentle and thoughtful.' She gazed at his green eyes, touching his hair.

'They have to make you feel special too and I make you feel special I hope,' he said. 'I am hungry and I want the food now.' He started to scan the table. The food lay spread across the table with pastries to small plates and sweets to wire stands. She breathed a gasp of delight at a pink cake stacked high upon the table.

'What is happening with the bank vault,' she asked as she reached for the cake.

'I have got the script from Jonnie Suliam, the meeting was a success,' he said passing around the table.

'Well done, Denem,' she said, following him.

'I will access the vault this evening, I require the laptop.' He grimaced at her. 'I am going to access the funds.' He wanted Stephanie there. He looked across at a waiter, and raising a hand, he cried for the laptop to be collected to the table. Pushing the plates to one side, he made room for the device to be placed before him. The thin waiter rushed to him.

'Get me an iced lollipop for this,' she demanded as the waiter placed the laptop to before them with the screen open, ready for him to type. He inserted the keyring into the computer and the long number appeared on the screen.

'Is it necessary that you eat those now,' he said.

'I will eat an iced lollipop at the table as you work.' She turned to the iced lollipops and annoyingly grasped one in her small hand. She pointed her finger across to him and then at the laptop. 'I will pass you an iced lollipop if you want and you may enjoy one with me,' she said.

'I am to focus upon this for a moment and then I will continue with you,' said Denem angrily, as he strained his eyes at the screen viewing the figures before him. The screen flashed and the large sums of money began to fill his account. He had achieved his dream. The bank balance rose in value.

'Join me, Denem,' Issy whined, trying to distract him. He considered Stephanie as the money downloaded.

'I don't want a lollipop but I will take that one from your mouth to your body later on this evening.' He grinned and grabbed her hand in excitement at what he was viewing to the screen.

'I have done it. I have the funds, this is a great day.' He clapped his own hands.

'You are good, Denem, but I want to get all sticky to reward you,' she said. 'That is how I will be for you later on.' She annoyingly raised the iced lolly to her mouth.

'We are to eat food you don't want to eat a lollipop now,' he suggested to her, closing the laptop. 'We'll try to have fun with them later.'

'Tell me about your other work,' she said, dropping the lollipop onto a plate before her. It began to melt.

'I am also undertaking several buildings with funding from Suliam,' he said as they moved towards the cake. 'We copied the tower blueprints.' He pointed to the large pink fondant cake with piping on the table. 'Shall we begin with this cake,' he said bitterly.

'You are so good, Denem.' Unaware of how he was feeling she gazed at him through blue eyes. She began thinking about all of the money that she had witnessed tranfering to his accounts. She tilted her head to him. 'Have we found love?' she asked.

'Love is one thing but remembering each other when we are apart is another.' He wondered how long that they would actually be together because he missed Stephanie.

'Remembering each other when we are apart is important, we talk, we touch, we share moments together and they should be remembered,' she said excitedly, changing the subject from his work.

'I remember you when we are apart,' he said laying his hands on her. 'Don't worry about that.' She turned and smiled at him touching his solemn hair in place.

They began the cake at the table and reaching forwards, Denem collected a globule of fondant on his finger, taking it to his mouth.

'I would like to sit to the courtyard beyond.' She pointed with a long elegant finger to the courtyard filled with long grass and brown entwined wicker furniture. The garden held flowers beside bushes dotted with red berries.

'Take the meringues with us,' she asked.

He viewed the meringue stand holding swirling meringues. They were on the rack in pink and white and with high peaks. He signalled to the waiter to collect the rack. Issy watched him carefully as he moved from the room to the terrace. He passed through the doors turning to her and smirking from his angular face. A fountain before the doors of the garden had fish and white floating lily flowers. He strode to the fountain and stooping forwards, he viewed the koi fish moving through the swirling pool.

'The fish are swirling in the pool, come and take a look at them,' he said pointing down at the water.

'They are shiny it is as if they are glowing,' she said with wonder.

'They are white and are reflecting the light from the sky, they are beautiful,' he said, placing his large hand on the edge of the fountain. 'There are so many of them.'

'It is mesmerising I could sit and view these all day.' She gazed at the reflecting pool for a moment, before standing and moving to the table. She smiled as she viewed the meringues to position the plate before her. Sitting, she took the meringue with her silver fork.

'Take a meringue with me.' She raised the fork and ate the sugary delight. She tilted her head, crumbs of meringue stuck to her lips, and with a raise of her hand she touched her lips with long fingers, removing the white crumbs of sugar.

'Are you enjoying them?' said Denem.

'Talk to me like you do, Denem, as I eat these,' she said gazing at her plate, at the crumbly mess.

'We could consider how truthful we are with each other and what it means to be truthful,' he said. 'Do you think that you are innocent, Issy?'

'Innocence is held with those that are true, and I am true,' she said lowering her fork and gazing at him wide-eyed.

'We are innocent if we are true and good with each other. That is what counts between people,' said Denem beginning to consider Stephanie and wondering where she was. He enjoyed speaking to her in this way. Several weeks had passed and they had not been together.

'That is what keeps us together, Denem. We don't blame each other for things if we are true to each other,' said Issy, viewing him.

'We are meant to want only what is the best for each of us, but sometimes that is difficult,' he said dismissively. He stood and took a step beside a stone wall, covered with small white wall flowers, that grew and flourished between the small cracks. He collected several of the flowers from the rock garden in the palm of his large pale hand, and then laid them to rest on the table, unfurling his heavy fingers to show her the flowers. She rested her arm on the back of the chair and began to stand, craning her neck to view the flowers resting on the white table cloth.

'Are they a gift?' she asked eagerly.

'The flowers are a gift from me to you,' he replied, begrudgingly.

She moved to him and grasped his covered arm tightly, feeling the fine, soft, white cotton with her elegant hands.

Chapter 22
Dan

A black painted ornate streetlamp shone light that fell over the pavement. Lush green leaves held a circular reef to the door. He stood gazing at the white stucco house with large decorative French windows. Aston stood beside him in unkempt taut trousers wrapped around his legs and clinging to his ankles, revealing a large slovenly black boot. A ragged dark grey shirt clung to his lean, toned body, which he wore above a shabby suit jacket. The door that they approached was dimly lit by a lamp at its side, a large blue door, adorned with heavy weight ironmongery. Denem arrived at the front of the building first, and exited his vehicle. Aston stood before the open door of the large black car.

'She is inside the property. Shall we make our way through the door or shall I call to her.' Upon seeing Denem arrive, from the window of the house, a black male acting as an aide to Dan knocked on the door to the bedroom. Stephanie stood inside partially dressed, with Dan standing, wearing fitted jeans and an elfish soft hooded top, with a large hood that hung down his lean back. He demanded privacy.

'We are busy in here, can this wait,' he shouted aggressively.

'Go away,' she said turning her head to scream at the door with a lustrous voice. She bent over the high solid dark walnut sideboard that ran the full length of the living room. Her fingers were flared and her hands pressed hard against the timber surface, as he pushed towards her body, she could feel the cold sideboard against her naked flat chest. A tall, sleek woman., she had a slender, bony figure. She had seduced a great number of men through her life and they had fallen for her charms, her long limbs had entwined great numbers for Denem. Her thick full head of hair was brown and smile lines adorned her cheeks. Above her high cheekbones, large, elliptical blue eyes filled her face.

'Leave us alone, you know that we are busy,' Dan demanded.

'Push it into me,' she said in a silky voice. 'I want it deep, let me feel it, right here,' she said signalling to her lower stomach. Her mouth opening slightly as he met her with his body. She slapped an open hand aggressively onto the sideboard in demand.

'Have it, take it all,' his voice soaring, he responded on the tip toes of his training shoes, pushing as high into her as he could.

'I cannot feel it, where is it?' She could feel it high inside of her but she wanted him to feel inadequacy, she could easily take more. She closed her eyes to concentrate and thought about Denem. His green captivating eyes and his large sturdy pale hands. 'I want more,' she shouted with an excited shrill to her voice. He continued to thrust away at her from behind.

'Do you like it?' Dan's deep voice asked, in the hope of satisfying her. His blithe, red, soft-soled shoes finished to a thin dark jean trouser.

'Give me more,' she screamed a lustrous scream shaking her head from side to side as she looked down towards the floor between her legs. Her hair was ruffled and fell in long curls in front of her face. She wore a small pair of cotton pants and her tight skirt was pulled to her knees, she stood barefooted with her expensive wedged soled shoes sat beside her, kicked from her feet. She turned her head to look back over her shoulder at the thin man that stood behind her.

'I am doing it Stephanie. I am doing it,' breathed Dan, his

voice soaring as he struggled to satisfy her. He wore on his light body, a hooded top, with a large puckish number four emblazoned on its front. He continued to push at her with force, he was stood upon the tiptoes of his red soft-soled shoes thrusting his hips forwards against her, in an attempt to get to her.

'Shut up. Do not speak to me,' she ordered in a silky voice. Shutting her eyes, she imagined Denem passing deep inside her. The tall figure towered over her and he remained fully dressed in his hooded jumper and jeans. He had allowed little time to remove his clothes and he felt warm and under continued pressure to perform, small beads of perspiration had begun to appear upon his forehead.

'Slow down with me, you are going too quickly,' her deep gravelly tone passed, her head rocked back and the elongation of her neck became pronounced and her voice box raised from her neck. 'Strong deep movements, more slowly,' she demanded, banging her foot onto the ground. He rose to his tiptoes once more and pushed as high as he could.

'Have that,' he said again in a high tone, this time reaching forwards with his hand to grab at her hair in excitement.

'Get off of my hair,' she screamed. He immediately released the grip on her hair and removed his hand allowing it to drop back to his side. She was unhappy with Dan, she had missed the long days with Denem and no one was to touch her hair.

'What,' he replied startled by her response.

She closed her eyes and concentrated. She chose to face away from him he could have been anyone and she allowed her imagination to take control of her, through grabbing at her he had broken her concentration. In an attempt to regain composure, she continued. 'Reach as far into my body as possible,' she screeched. As she spoke, there was a knock at the door, and Dan's aide entered the room.

'Excuse me, Dan,' he said nervously from the open door knowing that he was interrupting. They ignored him and he continued angrily. 'You should know. Denem has arrived downstairs, and he is on his way up to see her. If he catches you like that he will not be happy.'

'Get out, I am not with him. He does not choose to visit me often enough,' she said, uncurling a long, nailed finger and pointing it towards the door. She swallowed in search of saliva but her mouth was parched and dry.

Denem lifted his arm, his blue blazer sleeve held closed with gold buttons and his thin gold watch shimmered from his sleeve. He entered the house with Aston's skeleton keys and then calmly made his way through the narrow, dimly-lit wallpapered corridors, to the bedroom. Denem had been visiting Stephanie at her home for a number of months, he had sent her to Dan to allow him to make contact with him for the retrieval of the script but Dan had not had access to it. Instead, he had kept Stephanie as his girlfriend and Denem wanted her back. He entered the room and pushed the unexpected aide that had entered to inform her of his arrival to one side. Denem stood in the doorway beside them and looked towards Stephanie.

'Why have you chosen to enter into relations with Dan, you were sent for a reason,' he said calmly.

'I do what I want, Denem, you don't care for me enough,' she said in a silky voice.

Stephanie stood partially dressed and stooped over the sideboard, he looked her up and down with a small smile. Dan removed himself from her body and quickly pulled on his jeans, at the shock of the entry to the room. He was covered and began to ready himself for the argument.

'Get out of here, Denem, we are busy,' he said with his voice soaring.

'I want the girl, she is with me,' Denem bellowed.

'You are going to sit down and speak with us, Dan, whether you like it or not,' Aston said. His sharp cheekbones covered with sturdy, pale skin, had shabby small scars and scratches on his ragged mottled solid cheeks. His hair was shaved short and his shiny skin was smooth and burnished. He released a gun from a shoulder holster inside of his jacket and placed it under the chin of Dan, pointing the weapon towards the ceiling.

'You can take a step back, also,' said Denem with a meaningful whisper into Dan's aide's ear. 'Get on the floor over there or he will point the gun at you.' The aide dropped to one knee slowly making his way to the floor. He took a few steps into the room before dropping flat onto the carpet. Stephanie stood slumbered over the sideboard and she slowly turned her head to look towards the sound of Denem's voice.

'I don't have to go with you, but I will sit and speak with you, we could take a coffee, I am finished here.' She turned in her slumber to face the door to find Denem standing in the doorway. She took a staggered step to one side and steadied herself with her hand on top of the walnut sideboard. She looked at the aide before turning her gaze back towards Denem and dropping her eyelids to look at him seductively. He gazed at her heavy brown loose hair falling in curls across the strong structure of her long face.

'We should drink our coffee over there,' She said looking over her shoulder towards a small side table, hitching down her skirt. She dressed and then moved across the bedroom.

'Get her attention for the coffee,' said Denem gesturing towards the waitress as he pulled up a chair in the corner of the room at the round table. He felt drawn to her and he had enjoyed their relationship. He had missed her.

'You are familiar to me, of course you are, we have known each other many months. I have seen you regularly but I am not sure where you have been, that is why I invited myself here,' said Denem. Stephanie waved over her shoulder at the waitress to get her attention.

The waitress brought a trayful of coffee to the table. A small jug of cream stood on the table, and lifting the jug, he offered to pour some into Stephanie's cup. He hovered the jug over the cup.

'Shall I pour the cream for you?' he said.

'You may.' She took the spoon and catching the cream as he poured, she smirked at him. She then took the spoon into her mouth and sucked the cream from it. She paused for a moment her eyes were stern and serious. She slowly dropped the spoon between her legs and it disappeared. She collected a small biscuit from the plate and broke it in two, taking a small amount into her mouth.

'There is crumb on your lip,' Denem said, and with large hands took the serviette from the table and passed it across to her. She took it from his hand and dabbed her lip gently removing the crumb. She held the serviette in her hand for a few moments before raising it with her hand and flinging it on the tabletop.

'Do you eat cheesecake?' He pushed a plate of cheesecake away from him with his fingertips.

'The best place to eat cheesecake is The Grestley, they do a fantastic cheesecake with a very deep topping and it is the perfect consistency. We could meet there next time, if you like,' she said.

'That would be great, we should take a room there and I will cover you in it,' said Denem. The woman smirked and reached down below the table with her hand. She moved her head to the side, gesturing for Denem to look below the table.

'When things happen, they are hidden. Take a look,' she said. Her large rounded piercing blue eyes fluttered at him from deep within the frame of her face. He looked beneath the table, and as he did so, she revealed her teaspoon that she had clutched clumsily in the palm of her hand. With her other hand she hitched up her skirt. It pulled tight across her legs. She ripped her knickers to one side, with the same hand she tucked the spoon into knickers.

'Give me the spoon. Dan will be back in a moment, we can do this later. I have to speak with him,' he bellowed.

'No.' She removed the spoon from her knickers, and then reaching across the table placed it onto his saucer.

'You are dirty.'

'You said, it was fine. I can be with whoever I like, and now you are collecting me from here.' She dropped her chin and brown curls fell forward across her cheeks. 'I will come with you when you leave.'

Dan returned to their side with his long hair curling across his forehead. They both paused to look at Dan as he pulled up a seat beside them.

'He is flirting with me, Dan, and I am letting him take me back,' she said.

'Then you can go with him, you don't need to be here any more.' He lifted a slim hand from a hooded jumper to signal to Denem that everything was fine.

'As long as everything is OK, Dan, I don't want to leave here with you too upset.'

'I'm not upset, Denem, I have got plenty of women.' Dan relaxed into his chair beside them.

'I will take her then, you are coming with me,' Denem bellowed lifting a pale hand and resting it on the table before them. He turned his green captivating eyes upon her.